What the Gulls Were Singing

Cover painting by TED LEWIN

Body illustrations by JACK SMITH

What the Gulls were Singing

Phyllis Reynolds Naylor

FOLLETT PUBLISHING COMPANY
Chicago   New York

The verse on page 15 is from "The Wanderer," from *Complete Poems* by Eugene Field, published by Charles Scribner's Sons, New York, 1910.

Library of Congress Catalog Card Number: 67-21163

FIRST PRINTING

Follett Publishing Company
1010 West Washington Boulevard
Chicago, Illinois 60607

T/L 9265

Contents

What the Gulls Were Singing

To Rex and our ocean

1

Ghost in the Gables

The moon was on the water and sand was in the wind. As Marilyn stepped out of the car into the darkness, she could feel the grit on her teeth. It stung her cheeks and eyelids.

Father's dream house looked like something haunted. All that Marilyn could see was a big black blob on a hill. All she could hear was the howl of the wind around its gables and the low roar of the ocean as it rolled lapping up on the beach.

It will be different here, Marilyn thought. Maybe it

would turn out that Nico, when he came, had always wanted a kid sister. Maybe even Peter would change. But somehow things would be different. Marilyn just knew it.

"I'll carry Ricky," Mr. Buckley said, reaching into the car for the baby.

Marilyn flung herself across the sandy lot beside Peter and Danny, her long red hair wild in the wind. Peter reached the house first and fumbled with the lock.

Creeeeeak, went the door as he pushed it open.

"Oh, Peter, it's spooky!" Marilyn breathed, peeking inside.

"It smells spooky, too!" whispered Danny.

Mother came up on the porch behind them and flicked on the light.

The Buckley family stood in the center of the big straw carpet and looked about the room. Everything in it was old and smelled of the sea. There was a fireplace on one side, its mantel covered with dusty shells. A rose-colored couch and some wicker rocking chairs were piled beneath the windows, and a captain's bell, mounted on a stand, sat in one corner. There were doors to the bedrooms and kitchen and a staircase leading to the rooms above.

"Two more floors," Peter yelled, halfway up the stairs. "I'm going to explore."

"Me too," said Marilyn.

Four-year-old Danny took Marilyn's hand and warily climbed the stairs. "If I see any ghost, I'm gonna . . . gonna bite his leg," he declared.

10

There were eight bedrooms and four baths on the second floor, and six bedrooms and two bathrooms on the third. Every bedroom on the top floor had a gable.

Crouching down at a front window on the third floor, Marilyn and her brothers pressed their heads against the screen. The waves rolled in off the big black ocean— *ssslish, ssslish*— the salty air sneaked up their noses, and occasionally a gull, which should have been asleep, called out sharply in the night sky above them.

"Do you think you'll like it here?" Marilyn asked Peter.

"Of course! Won't you?"

Marilyn nodded without answering. Peter was always so sure of himself. She didn't know yet just how she felt about the ocean. Too much depended on people.

The boarding house was Father's idea. Every year, from September till June, he taught high-school English. For a long, long time, he'd dreamed of having a house on the ocean for his family to live in during the summer. They would take in boarders to help pay the cost, and this way they would get a vacation at the beach every year—all summer long. Now they had the house. All they needed were boarders.

Marilyn was about to turn away from the window when suddenly her eye caught a glimpse of something in the yard below.

"Peter! Look there!"

"What?"

"I saw it . . . just a minute ago," said Marilyn.

Again the dark clouds rolled off the moon for a moment, illuminating the ground.

"There!" said Marilyn.

Something, or somebody, was standing in the front yard, motionless, looking up at the house. But before Marilyn could make it out, the shadows closed in again and the yard was dark.

"Come on. Let's go down on the balcony," said Peter.

They raced down the hall to the side stairs and on down to the second floor. There a door opened onto the balcony above the front porch. Peter and Marilyn, with Danny clutching at their clothes, hurried outside and around to the front.

The yard was empty.

"But we *saw* it!" Marilyn whispered.

"A ghost!" said Peter, almost eager, and Danny started to cry.

"Shhhh," Marilyn told him. "Whatever it was, it's not in the house."

They went back inside and heard Mother calling them from below.

"Anybody hungry?"

They trooped downstairs and into the kitchen.

"Daddy, something was out in the front yard. We saw it," said Marilyn.

"What?"

"I don't know . . . it looked like a ghost. It was just standing there and then it was gone."

Mr. Buckley frowned. "I don't want any more talk of ghosts. You're going to have Danny scared stiff."

"Well, I want a bedroom on the top floor, right in front," said Peter, hoping to see it again.

"We'll see," said Mother, passing out sandwiches and apples. "Maybe . . . since you and Nico will be sharing one. . . ."

"Who's Nico?" asked Danny. "Is he a ghost?"

"He's the boy who's coming to live with us this summer," Mrs. Buckley explained.

"I want a front room, too," said Marilyn.

"Now wait a minute," said Mr. Buckley. "Those are the best rooms. We've got to save them for boarders. Maybe Peter and Nico can have one, but not you, Marilyn."

"Why?" Marilyn clunked down her glass. "Why does Peter get one then?"

"Marilyn, be reasonable," said her father. "It's not just for him, it's for Nico. We want the boy to like it here."

"I wanna sleep with Peter, too," Danny said.

"Oh, stop it, all of you," said Mrs. Buckley wearily.

Danny slowly bit into a peanut butter sandwich, and looked around at the other members of his family—all red-haired except Mother, whose hair was brown. Mr. Buckley was growing a beard, and his red whiskers stuck crazily out on his cheeks and chin.

"You look like a pirate, Daddy," Danny giggled.

"I don't feel like a pirate," his father smiled. "I feel like a beachcomber—a happy, carefree beachcomber." He turned to Mother. "Remember that poem, Pat, about the ocean?

" 'Upon a mountain height, far from the sea,
    I found a shell,
And to my listening ear the lonely thing
Ever a song of ocean seemed to sing,
    Ever a tale of ocean seemed to tell. . . .' "

Marilyn sat glowering at the table. *Always* Peter got what he wanted. Always, always, always. . . .

A big gust of wind howled fiercely around the house on the hill, rattling the door and whistling in under the windows. And suddenly, from upstairs, came a *thud, clumpity, thud, thud.*

Danny sat straight up, his cheeks as red as his hair and his eyes almost as big as his ears. "The ghost!" he exclaimed.

And then the lights went out. Danny yelped.

"A power line must be down," said Mr. Buckley. "I'll get a flashlight from the car." He groped his way to the front door. The wind banged it against the wall when he opened it, and Ricky cried. Mother picked the baby up and stood rocking him in the darkness.

"I found two flashlights," Mr. Buckley said when he returned, handing one to Peter. "You and Marilyn can go choose your rooms."

The stairs looked a lot longer, the shadows a lot bigger, as Marilyn went back up again behind Peter. If the ocean was going to change everything, it certainly

15

hadn't done it yet. Peter went right ahead getting every-thing he wanted because he was a boy, Father's favorite, and one lousy year older.

She waited silently while Peter chose one of the two front bedrooms on the third floor. He made up his bed and then handed the flashlight to Marilyn.

"Mar's got a mad on," he said mockingly. "You always want everything I do, Mar. That's the trouble."

"I do not," Marilyn snapped. She tramped down the hall to the bedrooms at the back, chose one, and slammed the door.

She stood there for a moment, shining the light in all the corners, listening to the roar of the wind around the gables. Finally she propped the flashlight up on the dresser and began making her bed. Each movement of her arms cast spidery shadows on the wall. Her heart beat faster, and as soon as she had slipped on her gown, she dived under the blankets, taking the flashlight with her and tucking it under her pillow.

A few more days and Nico would be here. None of the family had ever seen him. Nico was from Greece. If all went well, Father would adopt him and he would become one of the Buckleys. Marilyn imagined what he would be like—a big, smiling boy who loved to tease his kid sister and liked to have her around—the kind of big brother she'd always wanted, definitely *not* like Peter.

Thud, clumpity, clump, clump . . . went the shutters or the ghost, whichever it was. Marilyn went to sleep with one hand on the flashlight.

16

2

Goat on the Boardwalk

Marilyn flung open the screen door and raced down the steps. A light fog rolled off the ocean and she could just make out a ship on the horizon. Then she saw her father down by the water.

She kicked off her shoes and ran across the scrubby yard to the high bank which separated the Buckleys' house from the beach. With a yell, she tumbled down the side and sank ankle deep in the sand below. She couldn't stay angry forever.

"Up already?" Mr. Buckley called out. "Just smell

17

this air!" He stuck his hands in the pockets of his white pants, threw back his head and closed his eyes, smiling at the sun.

Marilyn had never seen him look so happy. Both she and her father had "freckle-specked noses" as Mother called them, and Marilyn even had freckles on her ears. But Marilyn had something more: she had one green eye and one gray eye.

"Daddy, why is sea water salty?" she asked, catching up with him. They sloshed along at the edge of the water where the tide left a white bubbly foam on the sand.

"I don't know," he answered. "Why do you have one green eye and one gray one? That's just the way it is."

That's just the way Father was, too. If Marilyn asked her mother, Mrs. Buckley would try to find out. Mother was practical and businesslike. If she didn't know the answer she would look it up.

But not Father. All Father wanted to do with sea water was put his feet in it, feel it, and remember how it felt long after he went back to school in the fall. That's just the way he was.

Ahead, a young woman was picking up driftwood and putting it in her skirt. She straightened up when Marilyn and her father approached and smiled broadly.

"Hello," she called.

"Good morning," said Mr. Buckley. "Nice day, isn't it?"

The lady nodded. "Every day is nice at the ocean."

She was a strange-looking woman, and Marilyn found herself staring. Despite the heat of the sun, she was fully dressed, except for shoes. She wore a full brown skirt that came halfway to her ankles, and an old blue jacket which was much too tight. Her hair was very long and very black, and as the wind tossed it about, Marilyn could see the glint of gold earrings in her ears. Her brows were thick, and her skin was brown and weathered, like finely crumpled paper. She looked as through she had lived out here on the beach in the wind and the rain all her life, like a fence post.

The young woman smiled again. "I am Cassandra." She said it as though everybody who had ever been to the ocean knew Cassandra because she was part of it.

"We're the Buckleys," Father said. "Just bought that house up there. Want to take in boarders—see if we can make a go of it."

"Ah!" Cassandra nodded. "That's a fine house." She stood looking up at it a moment. Then she shifted the driftwood about in the big fold in her skirt. "I sell this on the boardwalk in the evenings. Perhaps you would like some?"

"I'll talk to Pat," Father grinned. "She's looking for things to spruce up the living room."

With a friendly good-bye to Marilyn, Cassandra moved nimbly on down the beach in her bare feet, her full skirt swaying from side to side and her long black hair blowing all around her head.

20

"Is she a gypsy, Daddy?" Marilyn asked, looking after her.

"It's hard to tell here at the ocean," said Father. "We're all gypsies at heart."

From the front porch, Marilyn could see in three directions. To the left, the beach was rocky and tufted with weeds. To the right, beyond a vacant lot, the boardwalk began and ran along the busiest part of the beach. Straight ahead lay the ocean.

But exploring would have to wait. All morning long Marilyn and Peter helped clean the house. The rooms had to be vacuumed, the windows washed, and the beds made up.

In the afternoon, Father began work on a big sign. It said:

BUCKLEYS' BOARDING HOUSE

Reasonable Rates—Daily, Weekly, Monthly

The three children sat on the back porch watching. Mother brought the baby out and put him in Marilyn's lap. "Would you hold him while I wash the windows? I think he'll like being out here in the sun."

Marilyn rocked Ricky gently in her arms. Eight months old. He was such a funny little baby—with soft orange fuzz for hair. He always looked so sleepy, and

21

sounded like a little mouse when he cried.

Danny stuck his peach in the baby's face.

"Get that out of here," Marilyn scolded.

"Can't I even give him a bite?"

"Of course not! He doesn't have any teeth!"

Danny peered in the baby's mouth. "He looks like Grandpa. He's only a little boy and he looks like an old man."

"Well, he's little, and he has to be handled gently," Marilyn said, shifting the baby to her shoulder. "You always do such dumb things."

Danny glared at her. "*You* always get to take care of him! *You* always get to do *everything*!"

"Look!" Mr. Buckley put down his paint brush. "Do we have to have fussing every single day of the year? Do you think anybody's going to want to stay here and listen to that all the time?"

"Whenever there's a quarrel, Mar's in it," Peter said.

"That's enough!" Father told him. "You do your share, too!"

Well, thought Marilyn, big old Smarty Peter finally got a kick in the pants. She looked at him, perched up there on the railing. Eleven years old, he had big eyes and sort of bony cheeks. But he was handsome. With everything else, Peter had to be the best-looking one in the family besides.

"When's Nico coming, Dad?" Peter asked.

"Tomorrow. If I thought you and Marilyn could ride to Baltimore and back without fighting, I'd take you to the airport to meet him."

Danny sat down on the steps and sucked his thumb. "Why can't I go?"

"Because, little boy, your mother thinks you'll need a nap, and it's a long drive there."

Danny continued sucking his thumb. "Why do we got to have more children?"

Father glanced over at him, grinned, and went on painting.

"Sometimes I wonder myself," he said. "Particularly when the three of you get to quarreling. But it just so happens that your mommy and I like kids. And now that we've got four of our own, we thought we'd finish our family off by adopting some from other countries."

"You mean you'll get some more after Nico?" Marilyn asked excitedly. "A girl?"

"We'll see, we'll see," said Father. "One at a time. I never did want twins, you know."

There were hurried footsteps in the kitchen, and Mother burst through the back door.

"We've got our first boarder!" she said. "A woman wants to stay all summer!"

Mr. Buckley wiped his hands. "Wonderful! Sign her up."

"Are we taking pets?" Mother asked.

"Why not?"

"Well, this is a goat."

"A *goat*?" said Father.

"A *goat*?" screamed the younger Buckleys, and the

23

whole family crowded back into the house to see this remarkable pet.

Miss Tugberry looked as though she were ninety-nine years old. She wore a big straw hat and a green dress with ruffles on the sleeves. And she was holding the leash of a beautiful snow-white goat.

"How do you do?" said Father, shaking her thin hand. "I'm Ralph Buckley, this is my wife, Pat, and our four children. You have a most unusual pet there."

Miss Tugberry stroked the goat's head. "Sylvia and I have lived together for almost three years," she said. "She is a Saanen goat, the great-granddaughter of one of the finest Swiss goats in the country, and I'm not about to part with her now."

Father smiled. "I wouldn't think of turning away two such remarkable ladies. We'll make a place for Sylvia under the back porch. I know you'll like it here."

Sylvia had a silky pointed beard and bushy brows, and she wore a lavender collar with silver bells around her neck.

"Could I take her for a walk?" Marilyn asked, handing Ricky to Mother.

"Of course you may, child," said Miss Tugberry.

So Marilyn, holding the lavender leash, led the tinkling goat outside and across the long sandy lot to the boardwalk, with Danny prancing gleefully behind. People stared and pointed, and soon a crowd of children followed.

Sylvia stepped haughtily along, her head high, and

her neck stretched out toward the sun. Her little bells tinkled and she swayed from side to side, smiling a wry goat smile.

Down the boardwalk went the parade—Marilyn, Sylvia, Danny, and a crowd of giggling children. Past the auction house and fudge stall, past the drugstore and gift shop—while dogs yipped and waitresses came out to look and lifeguards turned and scratched their heads.

And then, right ahead, came a rumble of wheels and a toot and a whistle, and the little shuttle train, that traveled up and down the boardwalk, came into view. Its red and white awnings flapped in the breeze and its wheels went clackity-clacking over the cracks.

Sylvia stopped. Her left flank twitched and she jerked her head.

Toooooooot, went the train again, clackitying closer. *Toooooot!*

The goat twitched again. She lifted one hoof and clattered it down excitedly.

"It's all right, Sylvia," said Marilyn, stroking her head. "Take it eas. . . . ."

Toooooooot! shrieked the train, rumbling right up beside them. The goat jumped to one side, jerking the leash from Marilyn's hand. With a fantastic leap, she went galloping off down the boardwalk, her whiskers flying, her little bells tinkling, her lavender leash dragging, with Marilyn and a dozen children after her.

Sylvia may have been the great-granddaughter of one of the finest goats in the country, but she certainly wasn't behaving like a lady. Her white legs flew out in all directions as she clattered down the boardwalk.

"Please stop her!" Marilyn yelled frantically, but people only stared with gaping mouths. Danny had long since given up, and stood panting back by the umbrella stand.

Ahead on the boardwalk, Marilyn saw a row of six bicycles coming toward them. One of the riders saw the goat and yelled. Then he tooted his horn and the other boys did the same.

Sylvia skidded sideways, her ears laid back. Then she sailed right off the boardwalk into the thick sand, did an about face, and began galloping back down the beach in the other direction. Meanwhile, crowds hooted and waved, and big men in bright-colored sport shirts whistled.

As they neared the boarding house, Marilyn was afraid to look up. Old Miss Tugberry would probably never set foot in Father's house again.

She was in the front yard, all right, but she was laughing. And as Marilyn plopped breathlessly down in the grass, Sylvia, the goat, slowed to a trot. Finally, with white sides panting, she cantered over to her mistress and nuzzled her affectionately.

"Oh, my dear," said Miss Tugberry, dabbing at her eyes, "I should have warned you. Sylvia detests whistles and horns and such. But she always comes back."

Now she tells me, Marilyn thought. She didn't mind Miss Tugberry's laughter, but she did Peter's.

"Mar, you should have *seen* yourself!" he shrieked, leaning over the porch railing. "Running after a goat! That was a riot!"

Marilyn blushed deeply. "Shut up," she snapped, her teeth together. *"Just shut up!"*

Mr. Buckley gave her a quick frown. "Marilyn, don't be so touchy," he said, and then to Miss Tugberry, "Come in the house and rest now. We want you to enjoy every minute of your stay here."

3

Nico

Nico arrived the next day. The moment he stepped off the plane, Marilyn knew it was he.

Though he was a year and a half older than Peter, Nico was an inch shorter, but his shoulders and arms were broad and muscular. His hair was thick and black, and there was something about his face that fascinated Marilyn. At first she thought it was the blackness of his eyes, like two ripe olives. Or perhaps it was his finely-pointed nose. Then, when Nico smiled, Marilyn was sure that was it, for he had the biggest, whitest teeth she had ever seen—like a row of white buttons.

Mr. Buckley put one arm around Nico and squeezed him hard. "Welcome, Nico," he said. "We're so glad you're here."

Nico laughed a little. "I am looking for man with red hair," he said in English, "but I did not know there is red hair, too, on his face."

Mr. Buckley grinned and stroked his beard. "This is only a week old. Wait till the end of summer." He turned to Peter. "This is Peter. You two are going to share a room."

"Hi," said Peter, shaking Nico's hand.

"Hi," Nico answered, smiling.

"And this is Marilyn," said Father.

"Hi," said Nico again. And that was that.

On the drive back to the ocean, Marilyn glanced sideways at Nico. Funny about his smile. Now it was there, now it wasn't. She wanted to say something really great to make him like her, but she didn't know what. So she didn't say anything.

"Oh, Nico, we're *so* glad to have you," Mrs. Buckley cried, coming out of the house. She hugged him to her, and Nico blushed.

"It is good to finally arrive," said Nico. "Even by plane it is a long trip."

"Have you ever seen an ocean?" Danny asked.

The others laughed, but Nico was polite. "No," he said, "I have seen the sea but never an ocean."

"And you haven't seen *our* ocean," Danny crowed,

29

grabbing his hand and taking him down to the water.

The young Buckleys had been clamoring for an evening on the boardwalk. Mother had promised: when Nico came, she said, they would go.

So, with Miss Tugberry rocking gently on the porch and Sylvia scratching her neck against the chair, the Buckleys and the boy from Greece set out in the early evening for the boardwalk.

The whole town seemed to come down to the beach at night—old people bundled up with scarves, young people weaving in and out of the throngs on bicycles built for two, high-heeled ladies wrapped in furs, businessmen in white sport coats, smoking their big cigars.

The stores along the boardwalk were open late each evening, and the children bought popcorn. Father bought fudge, thick and buttery, and then cotton candy.

"This is for eating?" Nico asked as the feathery stuff tickled his chin.

"Yes, yes, go ahead!" Peter yelled delightedly, and Nico took a big bite. Everyone laughed at his astonishment when the mouthful dissolved into a sweet trickle.

Even Ricky joined in the fun, cooing and waving his arms from the stroller where he was propped against a pillow. Marilyn and her mother stopped to buy beach hats, and as they started off again, Marilyn put hers on Ricky's head. Everybody laughed—everybody except Mother.

"I don't want everyone staring at him," she said shortly, and Marilyn took the hat away. Mother was always afraid someone was going to see Ricky. What were babies for if not to look at?

"Oh, look, Daddy, there's that lady." Marilyn stopped and pointed. Beyond the arcade, in a folding chair in the sand, sat Cassandra, her driftwood spread in front of her. She did not call out to people as they passed, but sat smiling at the moving throngs, her long hair loose and blowing around her shoulders.

"Who is she?" asked Mother.

"Cassandra. She sells driftwood," Marilyn explained. "Let's go look at it, Mother. I think she's a gypsy."

"I'll go on with the boys," said Father, taking the stroller.

Marilyn and her mother walked over to where the strange young woman sat. Cassandra smiled, her eyes half closed against the sand that traveled in the wind.

Mrs. Buckley picked up a large piece of driftwood and turned it around.

Cassandra opened her eyes wider. "Do you like that one?"

"Very much," said Mother.

"Then you may have it for a dollar. It would look very nice on your fireplace."

Mother looked curiously at Cassandra as she paid her. "How did she know we have a fireplace?" she asked Marilyn as they left.

"Maybe she can just tell things like that," said Marilyn.

When they caught up with Father and the boys,

31

Mother said, "That woman's a witch, Ralph."

"Now, Pat—that's not something you'd like the kids to hear you say, is it?"

"But she's so strange! She looked like she knew all about us."

A witch! thought Marilyn. A Ghost in the Gables and a Witch on the Beach! What next?

"Oh, look, Mother, at the beautiful shell bracelets!" Marilyn breathed, stopping at a store window. "See that white one near the back? Oh, Mother, could I buy it, please?"

"It is pretty, honey," said Mother. "But three dollars is a lot. Wait until the end of the season, and you'll be able to buy one cheaper."

Everyone went on the ferris wheel, but Mother kept Ricky and Danny with her when the others got on the roller coaster. Marilyn and her father climbed in one seat, and the two older boys got in the one behind.

"Hold on tight, Nico," Mr. Buckley warned as the car started its slow climb. "Don't you boys try anything silly."

He needn't have worried. When the car reached the top and went rocketing down the other side, Marilyn thought she would not live to see it stop. Before she could catch her breath, it raced around a corner so violently that she bumped heads with Father. She tried to scream, but the force of the wind pushed back her lips and left her teeth dry. Up raced the roller coaster over another hill and plummeted down again.

"Good heavens, Nico, you're not sick, are you?" Mother called as the boy weaved off the platform beside Peter.

"I cannot understand people should pay to be knocked so apart," Nico declared. "They should pay me to go on the ride."

Everyone laughed.

It was fun being out at night. It reminded Marilyn of a time several years ago when she and Mother and Peter and Father would do things together. She and Mother would go down the hill on one sled, Father and Peter on another. Or she and Mother would take one path through the woods and Father and Peter another just to see who got home first. Back then, Mrs. Buckley had been Marilyn's very special friend. But that was before Danny and Ricky were born.

"Let's go walk down by the water," Mr. Buckley said. "Everybody take your shoes off."

"I'll meet you at home," Mother smiled, going on with Ricky. "Don't freeze."

Mr. Buckley and the four children stepped off the boardwalk and headed out across the sand toward the cold black ocean.

Mr. Buckley and Danny were running on ahead, and Marilyn was following behind Peter and Nico. They had only gone a short way when they passed a group of boys coming in from the water.

The boys wore swimming trunks and carried surf-boards over their heads. Their laughter was loud and show-offish, Marilyn thought, and their long hair had been bleached a light yellow.

"Look, Peter!" Nico said. "They do surfing here? That is something we do much in Greece!" He stopped to admire the boards, and it was then the boys noticed him.

"Hey!" said one of the boys. "Get a load of the Greek."

The others turned around.

"Real imported stuff," said another. "When did you get off the boat, kid?"

Nico looked puzzled. "I did not come by a boat," he said. "I came on the airplane. . . ."

"An air-o-plane!" one of the boys said contemptuously. "How 'bout that? Big stuff, huh!"

"C'mon, Nico," Peter murmured, starting on toward the water.

"Who's your carrot-top friend, Greek?" said another one, as the boys closed in. "Ain't you gonna be sociable?"

At that moment Mr. Buckley called, "You kids coming?"

The surf riders stepped back.

"The old man," said one, and they went on back up the beach.

"Oh, Daddy," said Marilyn, running up to her father. "Did you hear what those boys said to Nico?"

"I do not understand," said Nico. "In Greece, they are my friends, the ones with the surf boards."

34

"I'm sure you'll find some decent kids here, too," Mr. Buckley told him. "That was not our finest crop of Americans."

Danny reached the water first. "It's cold, Daddy!" he yelped. The others waded in behind him, enjoying the ooze of wet sand between their toes as they walked down the dark shore.

Down by the water, the noise of the juke box was faint and tinkling while the *ssslish, ssslish* of the ocean grew louder and stronger with each new breaker that rolled in.

Nico seemed to have forgotten the surfers, for his face was all smiles again as he sloshed along through the breakers.

"Look!" Father said suddenly. There, in a patch of moonlight, were a half dozen sand crabs, scurrying sideways on the tips of their claws and burrowing down into the holes where water bubbled up.

"They do not like to be away too long from the water," Nico said thoughtfully.

Marilyn looked at him through the darkness. He did not like to be away from the water either, she decided. He was far happier here than he'd been on the boardwalk.

4

Midnight Mystery

The Buckleys got another boarder. His name was Julius Green. He was not as old as Miss Tugberry or as young as Father, and he didn't bring anything with him but a black raincoat and a suitcase.

Father saw him one day down on the beach. He was standing perfectly still, staring up at the house as though he couldn't make up his mind.

Mr. Buckley went out in the yard. "Hello," he called cheerfully. "Can I help?"

Julius smiled. "You might," he said. "Got a room

for an old bachelor?"

"Only the best," Father said. "Come on up. Some day we'll get some steps on that bank and it'll make it easier for guys like us."

It was strange the way Julius looked around when he came in. It always seemed as though he were smiling, even when he wasn't. He chose a front bedroom on the second floor beside Miss Tugberry's.

"Do you like the house?" Father asked. "Ever roomed here before?"

"Roomed here?" Julius jerked his head around. "No . . . I've never roomed here." He picked up the pen and signed his name.

"It's really strange, Ralph, the way people seem to know this house," Mother said later. "First that young woman who sells driftwood . . . now Julius. . . ."

Father laughed. "Folks get attached to houses just as they do to people. Besides, it's a fine looking house. Why *shouldn't* they stop to stare?"

Geeek, geeek, geeek! Marilyn rolled over on the sand and squinted up at the sky where the gulls shrieked and nose-dived down to the water. She was so hot that the sand stuck to her arms and shoulders. Soaring above in the great white sky was a lot better than cooking down here in the sand like a baked potato, she decided.

Peter and Nico could have the water. She'd take the boardwalk any time. During the day she collected shells and other sea objects from the beach. At night, when neon lights flashed from store fronts, Marilyn took her basket of treasures and spread them out on the end of the boardwalk. Sometimes she found a "sea necklace"— the egg case of the conch—large leathery beads strung together in a row which held hundreds of teeny shells. She liked to break them open and show them to the people who stopped to look. Often she sold her shells for a nickel apiece.

"Marilyn! Why don't you come in?" Nico stood waist-deep in the water, yelling to her. Just as he opened his mouth to call again, a big wave rolled up behind and swallowed him up. A few seconds later his head popped back out of the water, and the wave slished on in, rolling all the way up the sand and lapping at Marilyn's toes.

It was nice to be asked, so Marilyn smiled bravely, tugged on her bathing cap, and ran splashing into the water. Ugh! How cold it was! Another breaker came roaring in and covered Nico. A moment later it got Marilyn.

Sometimes she escaped by ducking down under the water and letting the breakers roll over her. But this time she was knocked off her feet and pushed to the ocean floor in an icy somersault as a rush of water pounded past her ears. She scrambled coughing and spluttering to her feet, only to be knocked over again by another wave and scraped along the bottom.

It just isn't worth it, Marilyn muttered to herself. She waded heavily to shore and sank panting down on the sand.

Nico was teaching Peter to surf on a used board that Mr. Buckley bought for them. He made it look so easy. His strong, sun-browned arms paddled swiftly as a wave approached. As the board was lifted and hurled toward shore, he deftly climbed on top and guided it in by shifting the weight of his body. Then Peter would try, and if he managed to get on top of the board at all, he ended up beneath it long before it reached the beach.

"Always it takes practice," Nico would say, and they would try again. But they avoided the surf boys at the other end of the boardwalk.

Marilyn took off her bathing cap. It was hard to figure Nico out. Sometimes when he talked with her, he seemed to like her best of anybody in the family. Then he could turn right around and spend the whole afternoon with Peter, or take two hours molding tunnels in the sand with Danny.

She put on her sunglasses and had just rolled over on her back when she saw a figure standing above her.

"Oh!" she gasped, jerking herself up and looking into Cassandra's brown face.

"I hadn't meant to scare you," Cassandra said, sitting down beside her. "In sand, one can walk like the wind, for nobody will hear." She looked at Marilyn. "And how do you like the ocean?"

"I . . . I'm not sure, yet," Marilyn stammered.

"Ah! An honest girl!" Cassandra smiled. "Take your time, for the ocean will grow on you." She glanced up toward the big house. "And the boarding house. How is it going?"

"Well. . . ." Marilyn hesitated, wondering how much she should tell her. "We only have two boarders so far."

"Oh," said Cassandra. She was quiet for a minute. Then she said, "Young people, I suppose?"

"Oh, no. Just Julius and Miss Tugberry. Did you want a place to live, too?"

"No," Cassandra smiled. "I am here all year round, like the gulls. I have my own little house far down the beach past the pier. It is like a doll's house. Just one room. You must visit me some time."

Marilyn gulped. Mother would never let her go to a stranger's house alone.

Cassandra seemed to sense what she was thinking because she said, "Do come and bring anyone you like." Then she got up, smiled, and left, as noiselessly as she had come.

Evenings at the boarding house were quiet. The Buckleys, with Miss Tugberry and Julius, sat on the front porch talking and listening to the gulls or the sound of a foghorn. On down the beach, lights twinkled from cottages and tents. Up the beach, the other way, flashed the neon lights of the boardwalk. But straight ahead there was nothing but black, and the *ssslish, ssslish, ssslish* of the breakers.

One night after Marilyn had gone to bed, she heard

a creaking noise downstairs. She sat up. She could hear it distinctly now, the creak of the staircase between the first and second floor, and the soft thud of footsteps.

She squinted at the clock on her dresser. Eleven-thirty. Whoever it was went down instead of up, because shortly after the creaking stopped, she heard the front door close. For a few minutes she sat there without moving. Then she heard Peter and Nico tiptoeing out of their room and along the hall to the side stairs. They had heard it too. She waited until they had gone all the way down. Then she got up quickly.

When she reached the second floor, she opened the door to the balcony and edged her way toward the front. She looked over the railing at the darkness below.

A shadowy figure moved off the porch, crossing the front yard in the moonlight.

"Julius!" Marilyn whispered under her breath.

She watched while the man in the black raincoat crawled down the bank and onto the beach below. The minute he was over the edge, Nico and Peter darted out from the side of the house. They skimmed across the yard, crouching down on their hands and knees, the wind whipping at their pajamas. Marilyn watched, fascinated. What sort of a game was this?

Near the edge of the bank, the boys lay down on their stomachs where they could overlook the beach without being seen. But Marilyn, up on the balcony, could see everything.

Julius was walking out toward the ocean. He kept

going until he came to the big stump where Danny often played pirate. He stopped, looked around, and then knelt down and began digging in the little alcove on one side with both hands.

Marilyn stared. He was burying something! He reached in his pocket, took something out, and dropped it in the hole. Then he covered it up again and stamped on it.

Meanwhile, Peter and Nico began crawling backwards, and when they were out of sight of Julius, scrambled to their feet and ran, crouching, to the side of the house. They tumbled into the shadows just as Julius came up the bank. Marilyn almost laughed. The big detectives, and they didn't even know they were being watched.

She waited until she heard them come up the side stairs and go to their room. Then, after Julius had come back inside, she softly entered the balcony door, crept up to her room, and huddled shivering beneath her blankets, her nightgown cold from the wind.

Who was Julius, anyway? A spy?

She thought about Peter and Nico, and felt angry. They hadn't let her in on their secret. If Nico had been a girl, she would have shared a room with Marilyn. They would have laughed and giggled together and Marilyn, at last, would have something that Peter didn't. But that's the way it always was. Peter always had everything. It was Peter who got four *A's* and two *B's* on his report card last year. It was Peter who won second place

44

in the science fair. It was Peter who got the new bike, who got to go to New York, who never had to do dishes. . . .

"Peter's older," Mother always said, to explain it. But it didn't explain anything. Marilyn wished that just once, she could do something really great and exciting and wonderful, something Peter had never done. One thing she was sure of: she was going to find out what Julius had buried by that stump before the boys did.

Tap . . . tap tap tap . . . tap . . . .

Marilyn froze. It was not the thud and clump of shutters against the house or the wind around the gables. This was a knocking sound, and it seemed to come right from her wall. Her heart pounded.

Tap . . . tap tap . . . tap. . . .

Marilyn crawled down farther under the covers, her eyes wide open, straining to hear.

Tap tap tap . . . tap tap . . .

She scarcely breathed. What, or who, could it possibly be? Somebody trapped in the wall?

"W . . . who is it?" she said at last, her voice a whisper.

Tap tap . . . tap tap. . . .

"What do you want?" Marilyn asked.

But there was no answer. And though she listened for a long time, Marilyn heard nothing more but the faint *ssslish* of the breakers rolling in off the ocean.

5

Hurricane Watch

The next morning Marilyn tumbled out of bed, dismayed because it was seven o'clock and she'd wanted to be the first one on the beach.

As she ran downstairs, she saw Nico and Peter just going out the front door. At least they hadn't gotten there first.

As it turned out, however, nobody did any digging, for Julius was already on the beach, walking up and down.

For two days he either sat on the porch or walked

about the yard. He was the first one up in the morning, the last one to bed, and he finished his meals quickly.

Then one day Julius put on his hat and walked into town. The moment he was out of sight, Peter and Nico dashed out of the house to the stump. Marilyn ran after them.

"What do *you* want, Mar?" said Peter. "Go on. Beat it."

"I will not!" Marilyn retorted. "I happen to want to sit right here. What's the big secret?"

"None of your business. Go do something else."

Nico shifted uncomfortably. "Why do we not tell her, Peter?"

"You crazy? She'd blab it all over." Peter glared furiously at Marilyn and then, turning his back to her, dug rapidly so she could not see.

Nico did not help. He crouched glumly beside the stump, avoiding Marilyn's eyes.

"Blab it all over!" said Marilyn indignantly. "Listen, if you knew what. . . ."

Suddenly Peter stopped. He looked up at Nico. "There's nothing here. I've gone down two feet!"

Nico bent over the hole and dug too. There was nothing in the sand. Had someone come and taken what Julius had left? Was that why Julius had stopped waiting around?

Marilyn said no more. She was going to keep her secret about what she had seen, and watch Julius carefully. What's more, she wasn't going to tell anybody about the tapping in her wall, either. If Peter could have his secrets, so could she.

As the days went on, Marilyn was filled with curiosity. She trailed Julius to the drugstore. She peeked in his room when the door was open and watched him so closely at the table that Mrs. Buckley frowned.

"What in the world, Marilyn?" she said to her one night after dinner. "Haven't you ever seen a man with false teeth, for heaven's sake?"

That got Marilyn wondering. Maybe Julius had false hair, too. Maybe his eyebrows were false and his nose and his ears.

But Julius wasn't giving away any secrets. Each morning he strolled the beach. In the afternoon he sat on the porch and rocked and talked with Miss Tugberry. In the evening he put on a tie and walked into town to buy ice cream or a paper or to see a movie. It finally got so boring that Marilyn stopped following him. But she didn't forget.

It was the first day of July—rainy and cold with a dark sky overhead. Miss Tugberry's goat clattered around on the back porch maa-ing and twitching and carrying on as though a demon possessed her.

"At home, when a goat act this way, we would watch for the earthquake," Nico told Marilyn as he stroked Sylvia under the chin.

"And did it ever happen? Were you ever in an earthquake?"

Nico went on petting the goat. "Yes," he said, without looking up. "My parents were killed in an earthquake."

"Oh, Nico! I'm sorry. I didn't know that."

"It was a long time ago, but still I remember."

"What . . . what happened to you then?" Marilyn asked.

"I was visiting my aunt in Athens. When I found out about the earthquake in Volos, I never went back there. My aunt put me in a private school because she was not well enough to care for me herself."

"Did you like living at the school, Nico?"

The dark boy shrugged. "They were good to us and taught us many things. That was where I learn to speak the English. But . . . it was not like a home, you understand. I had a good friend there, but one day he was adopted. I did not think I would be. . . ."

"And then Daddy found out about you," Marilyn said brightly.

Nico just smiled.

Mrs. Buckley walked out on the porch holding Ricky and looked up at the sky. "Ralph says there's a hurricane out on the ocean that might get up here," she told them.

"A hurricane!" Marilyn cried.

"I will find Peter and ask him to help close the shutters," Nico said.

"That's a good idea, Nico." Mother put Ricky in his wooden cradle and quickly sat down to shell some peas, her eyes shifting occasionally to the sky.

"Will the hurricane hurt anything if it gets this far?" Marilyn asked, rocking the cradle with one foot.

"It could."

Sylvia, the goat, continued her restless pacing.

"Did you know that Nico's parents were killed in an earthquake?" Marilyn said, trying to make Ricky hold on to her finger.

Mother let a handful of peas fall into the pan. "I guess I didn't. We'd find all that out when we signed the final papers for him."

"When will that be?"

"At the end of the summer—when we see how he feels about us."

"You mean—he may want to go back to Greece?"

"That's a possibility." The peas made little tapping noises as they tumbled into the pan. "Or he just might not work out for some other reason. I hope he stays, because I like him very much."

Marilyn looked down at Ricky again. Suddenly she asked, "Mother, when is Ricky ever going to do anything?"

"Like what?" Mrs. Buckley asked sharply.

Marilyn glanced at her mother. Sometimes Mrs. Buckley seemed cross when anybody talked about Ricky. Marilyn couldn't understand it.

"Like . . . like sit up and crawl and . . . things other babies do," Marilyn said hesitantly.

Mrs. Buckley jerked at the pea pod in her hand.

50

"He's just an infant, Marilyn. He needs a lot of sleep."

Marilyn didn't answer. She looked back down at Ricky. Other babies didn't lie on their backs all day. Was something wrong with Ricky . . . something Mother didn't even want to admit to herself?

Crash! A terrible noise sent Mrs. Buckley leaping to her feet, and peas flew all over the porch. Peter and Nico came running out.

"Mom, that cracked window on the landing blew in and it's raining all over the floor!" Peter yelled. Mrs. Buckley picked up a mop and hurried up the stairs.

Mr. Buckley and Danny had been to the barbershop. When they came in, all wet and dripping, Danny held up a sucker. "Look what I have, Mommy," he yelled. "The man said he'd give me a sucker if he cut off my ears and he didn't cut them off and gave me a sucker anyway."

But Mrs. Buckley didn't laugh. "A window blew in, Ralph," she called.

Father shook his head. "The wind's terrible. But I talked to the men at the barbershop—they all think it won't amount to anything big—never does when it comes in July, they say."

Nevertheless, the rain continued to fall and the wind howled. The shutters on the gables rattled and shook even though they were shut tight.

The children put on their rain slickers and went out on the front porch. Father wouldn't let them go down by the shore. Sometimes, he told them, the storm

51

tide of a hurricane made the water rise several feet in a few seconds, and people had been swept out to sea.

The ocean front was deserted now. The clouds of water and sand that swirled above the beach looked like fog, and the great breakers that pounded the shore hissed and roared.

Mr. Buckley turned on the radio. There was no music now, and the announcer's voice was sober. Hurricane Donna was ninety miles away and heading right for the coast. She might slow down. She might turn out to sea before she hit. But no one could tell.

Father got some boards from the basement and nailed them across the front windows. The children carried in all the chairs and piled them in the living room. Mr. Buckley nailed the front door shut and came in the side entrance, the water running off the rim of his yellow rain hat.

There was nothing to do but wait. Julius poured the coffee and passed the pot around. Miss Tugberry held Sylvia's head in her lap, stroking the white hair of the goat with her long wrinkled fingers.

"It's a scary thing, I tell you," she said in her quivery voice. "When I was a young girl in Galveston, I saw the storm tide swallow up houses like matchboxes. Six thousand people lost their lives. It took my uncles and cousins, too. The roar of the water was like thunder!"

About four o'clock, the children went upstairs to look out the side windows, and came rushing back down again.

"The flags are up," Peter yelled. All up and down the beach, the frantic red flags with the black squares in the center warned that a hurricane was on the way.

The radio announced that the police wanted everyone to wait it out in the big brick high school. Mr. Buckley took Julius and Miss Tugberry and her goat first. Then he came back for the family. Ricky was crying.

"Look, Ralph, he knows something's wrong!" Mrs. Buckley said, holding the baby up and looking closely into his face. "He can tell!" Father patted her on the arm and they all climbed into the car.

That morning it had seemed exciting. Peter and Marilyn had never been in a hurricane, and each time the radio said it was coming closer, they whooped. But there was no laughter now—not after the look on Father's face. If anything happened to their house, it was the end of their summers on the beach—of the surf and the sand, the lights on the boardwalk, and hide-and-seek under the green, mossy pier. So far, there had been scarcely a penny to spare. If the house went, there was no money to build it again, for there was no insurance for houses along the ocean front. It was a gamble, and Mr. Buckley might lose.

Along with all the other families in town, the Buckleys and their boarders milled around the gymnasium, listening to the wind howling over the roof and eating sandwiches that the Red Cross passed around.

Cassandra was there. She saw the Buckleys and came over.

"That is a most beautiful goat," she told Miss Tugberry. "I have seen her many times as I walked along the beach. May I pet her?"

"Certainly," said Miss Tugberry, pleased.

Cassandra knelt down and began to stroke the goat when Danny yelled, "Don't let her, Miss Tugberry! She's a witch!"

"Danny!" cried Mother, horrified.

Danny looked bewildered. "But Mommy, you said so!"

Mrs. Buckley blushed deeply and Marilyn cringed with embarrassment. Cassandra gave a little laugh and went on stroking Sylvia. "I wish I were," she said. "If I were a witch, I would snap my fingers and the hurricane would go away—just like that."

"Do you live in this town?" Julius asked her.

"Yes—down by the shore. I am almost afraid to go look. . . ."

At five-thirty, the hurricane reached its peak. Power lines were blown down and radio broadcasts stopped. The force of the wind shook the walls, and the rattling windows clanked and banged.

Marilyn wandered out in the hall and peeked past a policeman, trying to see the storm outside. The four surf riders whom she had met on the beach the night Nico arrived were there, laughing and joking.

At that moment the wind blew out one of the glass panels in the door, and water cascaded through the hole and swirled down the corridor.

"Yahoo!" yelled one of the boys, holding out his arms as though he were riding in on the waves.

"Cut it out," said the policeman. "Get back inside, all of you."

"Hey, there's one of the carrot-tops," the tallest said as they moved back inside. "Where's your Greek boy friend?"

"He's not my boy friend," Marilyn said coldly. "He's going to be my brother. We're going to adopt him."

The boys jeered. "Hey, d'ja get that? Kid's old man must like Greeks."

"Yeah. Cheap labor," said another.

Marilyn scowled at them. What an awful thing to say! The more she saw of the four surfers, the less she liked them.

It was hard to wait out the storm. Now and then somebody would come in with stories of flying boards and bricks, but only a few men were allowed outside.

Danny and Ricky slept on the blankets Mother had brought, and occasionally Julius or Miss Tugberry dropped their heads with soft jerky snores. But the others couldn't sleep. Mr. Buckley paced up and down the hallways, talking to the men who came in from outdoors. No one could tell him about his house.

By morning, the hurricane had moved on. Now only a steady drumming of rain came down from the gray sky.

56

The Buckleys left Ricky and Danny with Miss Tugberry and went out. The street and yards looked like a dump. Boxes, boards, chairs, and shingles were strewn everywhere. Two cars on the corner had been overturned by the wind. The Buckleys found their car and moved slowly up the littered streets to the other end of town.

"I see our roof!" Mother cried, as they turned down the alley.

They climbed out, hurried through the back yard and up the steps at the side. Gingerly they climbed over the debris that covered the front yard.

Suddenly Father stopped, his long arms swinging helplessly at his sides. The front porch was gone, and part of the living room wall. With sinking hearts they made their way over the rubble and looked in.

The living room floor was covered with mud. The rocking chairs had been tossed about like toys. Sand was everywhere.

Mrs. Buckley's chin trembled as she bit her lip, and suddenly she grabbed Father's arm and leaned her face against his raincoat.

"Oh, Ralph," she sobbed. "First Ricky and now this."

Mr. Buckley put his arm around her and they moved on inside. Marilyn and Nico and Peter walked slowly back into the yard and stood looking down at the littered beach, the rain pattering down their backs. Marilyn fought desperately to hold back the tears, and finally

57

let them roll silently down her cheeks.

"It reminds me of Volos," said Nico. "I saw pictures of the town right after the earthquake. It was terrible."

Marilyn glanced at Peter. He looked as though he might cry too.

It was the end of Daddy's dream. It was all over before it really began. Why did people come to the ocean if they knew that hurricanes could blow their houses down? And what did Mother mean about, "First Ricky and now this?" Something *was* wrong with Ricky, but what?

She couldn't understand any of it. Everything seemed so different now. Even the gulls, screeching out their songs overhead, sounded melancholy and strange. Only the roar of the ocean was the same, and the breakers rolled steadily in, one after the other.

6

Cliff House

The sun shone the next day, but nobody noticed. The children made the beds and vacuumed the upper floors as usual, but no one went around to the front of the house and no one talked about it. Talking only made it hurt.

Finally Danny broke the silence. When he walked into the kitchen and saw his mother taking down the curtains, he said, "What are you doing that for, Mommy?"

Mrs. Buckley didn't look up. "Because we're going back home tomorrow," she answered.

"I thought we were gonna stay here all summer!" Danny said, not understanding, and when his mother made no reply, he grabbed her skirt and wailed, "I like it here, Mommy! I want to stay!"

"We all like it, honey, but we hadn't figured on a hurricane," his mother said. "There just isn't enough money to build the living room back up again. We're going to sell the house and go home."

Mr. Buckley reached out one big arm. "C'mon, boy, let's go down to the post office and get the mail."

Peter and Nico finished cleaning off the back porch and came in for a drink. Miss Tugberry helped Mother stack the dishes away.

"If there was anything I could do, Mrs. Buckley...," she said sadly. "We were having such a wonderful time here, Sylvia and I. . . ."

"We enjoyed having you, too," Mother said. "You're like a grandmother to the children. But. . . ."

There was a grinding of wheels in the alley, the slam of a car door, and Father came leaping up the back steps, waving a letter with Danny at his heels.

"Pat!" he yelled. "Stop packing! We're going to stay!"

Mrs. Buckley dropped a muffin tin. "How can we?"

Father thrust the letter at her. "We got a letter from an artists' colony in Pennsylvania. They want eight rooms from July tenth to August thirtieth. Eight rooms!"

"Oh, Ralph!" Mother grabbed Peter because he was the closest and hugged him hard. "That will pay for the

60

repairs! Oh, that's wonderful!"

"I wired them and told them I would hold the rooms," Father said, and then, jumping up, "To work! We'll have to really move to get everything done by the tenth."

The night before, the children hadn't been able to look at the wrecked living room without feeling their hearts sink down to their feet. Now, they couldn't look at the mud-caked furniture without laughing. The world was good again and they all felt silly.

Two chairs were upside down with the legs of one through the seat of the other, and this started the giggling. Mud covered the old upright piano, and everytime the children played a key, water squirted out, which made them laugh louder. Then Nico banged against the captain's bell in the corner and a clump of mud fell out and hit him on the head. The children howled.

Peter climbed up on the pile of chairs and lifted them off one by one while Nico and Marilyn carried them out in the yard to be hosed off.

"Hey, Mar, know what the day after tomorrow is?" he said. "Fourth of July."

"That is your national day?" Nico asked.

"Yep," said Peter, and suddenly he put the broom over his shoulder and sang, "Yankee Doodle went to town upon a horse named Hannah; fought a thousand troops and then he slipped on a banana."

Marilyn climbed up beside Peter and sang out even louder, "Yankee Doodle went to town, a-riding on a turtle; turned the corner just in time to see his mother's girdle."

Nico stared. "Those are strange national songs," he said, and Marilyn and Peter tumbled down shrieking with laughter.

Marilyn hummed to herself as she carried the chairs outside. Today Peter actually seemed to like having her around.

On the Fourth of July, everybody sat out in the front yard to watch the fountains and rockets go spinning off into the dark sky over the ocean.

"Do you have an Independence Day, Nico?" Peter wanted to know.

Nico nodded. "It is in March. The children wear blue and white clothes—the color of our flag—and there are parades. But we do not have fireworks. We save those for Easter."

"Easter?"

"Oh, yes. At night, bells ring and fireworks go off and everybody carries a big candle. We boil eggs and crack them against each other's."

"Oh, that would be fun!" said Marilyn. "Let's do that next Easter, Mother!"

"If Nico decides to live with us, he'll have a lot of things to show us," said Mrs. Buckley. She reached over in the darkness and put one arm around Nico, hugging him to her. Nico smiled, but did not answer.

The next day the workmen arrived. They poured

a new concrete porch instead of the old wooden one, and built back the wall and the roof. The hammering made Sylvia, the goat, uneasy, and Julius took her for a walk. The children tagged along. All up and down the board-walk, carpenters were pounding and sawing, and painters were making the mud-stained tourist houses white again.

At the other end of the beach, the pier rose above them on the sand. Dark and wood-smelly, it extended out over the water on its tall wooden legs which were covered with green slime. The children darted in and out among the pillars, looking up through the cracks at the workmen overhead, chilly in the dark eeriness.

Marilyn did not know what to make of Julius. He sauntered along in his white beach trousers like a kind old uncle. Who would guess that after the others went to sleep, he buried things in the sand?

"Sure lady, you can have that."

A workman's voice made them look up. The man was yelling to a woman on the bank who was holding a piece of board. It was Cassandra.

"All that wood is splintered," the man yelled. "Take all you need."

"Thank you," Cassandra called back. She bent over and loaded up her arms.

"We'd better go help," said Julius. He handed Sylvia's leash to Marilyn and walked over. "Can I assist?" he asked. "Where are you going?"

The sun-baked lady smiled at him, tossing the hair out of her eyes. "My house is . . . *was* . . . down there,"

63

she said, nodding toward the cabin with one side washed out. "I'm trying to build the wall back up."

"The boys and I can help," said Julius. "How about it, Nico. . . . Peter . . . think you can help carry this pile of wood down the bank there?"

"Sure," said Nico.

Cassandra turned to Julius as she stepped barefoot over the debris. "I believe I have noticed you on the porch of the Buckleys' house."

Julius nodded. "Yes. It is a good place to stay. The price is reasonable, Mrs. Buckley is a good cook, and," he added smiling, "the children are always in bed by eleven."

Marilyn saw Peter and Nico exchange glances.

Cassandra's little house had been hit hard. All the furniture had been moved out into the yard where it was cleaned and sunning, but one entire wall was still missing.

"Good grief!" said Julius. "Where have you been sleeping?"

Cassandra laughed good-naturedly. "Here. I have built back the wall many times." She sighed. "The wind and I are friends, but sometimes we quarrel. . . ."

"Quarrel!" said Julius. "Looks more like a knock-down drag-out fight! You must really love the ocean to put up with this."

"One learns to put up with a lot if he is truly happy," said Cassandra. "The ocean and I made our peace a long time ago."

64

Marilyn watched her curiously. What strange talk this was—making peace with an ocean. Quarrels with Peter she could understand. But quarrels with an ocean. . . .

"If you had a hammer and nails, the boys and I could help you put the wall back," Julius said.

"Please don't bother," said Cassandra. "I have done it before. It is a challenge, and I really like doing it. If I were a man, I think I would be a shipbuilder. I like making things with my own hands." She walked back up the bank with them. "Once my house has four walls again, you must all come to visit. Goat, too," she added smiling, stroking Sylvia's snow-white head.

As they reached home again, Nico gave Peter a nudge, for Julius had stopped and was looking quickly around, a strange look on his face. Suddenly Marilyn realized what had happened. The old tree stump on the beach was gone. The hurricane had lifted sand and earth from one place and piled it in another. It was impossible to tell now where the stump was buried.

No one said a word. Julius walked around and around, staring in all directions. Then he looked quickly at the children and said, "Well, let's get back to the house."

But something else was changed, too. Instead of an eight-foot bank leading up to the Buckleys' front lawn, it was now a fifteen-foot cliff. The hurricane had gouged out earth on the beach below and piled it on top of the bank. They all had to take the long way around to get back up to the house.

"You know," said Julius, when the procession marched into the kitchen, "I have a new name for your house, Mr. Buckley."

Father grinned. "Tell me quickly, because I'm about to paint another sign."

"Cliff House," said Julius. "The house is on a cliff, now that the hurricane has done its work."

"Yes, I noticed," said Father. "Hmmmm. Not bad! Cliff House, beside the sea. I like it."

Marilyn sat down on a chair and kicked off her sandals. "You know what, Daddy? We saw Cassandra picking up wood for her house. One whole wall is gone, just like our house, but she has only one room."

"That's terrible," said Father, shaking his head. "I guess we got off very lucky."

"Where does Cassandra live?" Mother asked curiously.

"In a cabin on the other side of the pier," Marilyn told her. "And now she is going to build it all back up herself."

"I think I'll bake something for her," Mother said. "You could take it over this afternoon, Marilyn. Tell her she's welcome to stay here until her house is repaired."

That afternoon, with Mother's cake under her arm, Marilyn set off for Cassandra's again. As she walked, she tried to imitate Cassandra's long steps and the willowy way she moved her shoulders.

When she reached the pier, she could hear the bang of Cassandra's hammer. Finally she came to the little cabin. The young woman was standing on a chair, pounding a board in place.

"Hi, Marilyn!" Cassandra called, giving the board a few more bangs and then climbing down. "See how much I've done already?"

"Mother said you could stay with us until it's finished," Marilyn said. "Here is a cake she baked for you."

"Why, how nice!" Cassandra unwrapped the chocolate cake and took a deep breath. "Ummmm. Sit down at my table, Marilyn, and we'll have a tea party right out in the yard."

She got a knife from the house and cut two thick slices. "Please tell your mother how much I appreciate it," she said. "And thank her too for offering your home. But I will have my bed back in by tonight."

Marilyn could think of nothing else to say. She sat nibbling politely on the warm cake, but the sun-browned lady didn't seem to mind the silence. She leaned back, watching the gulls circling overhead, her long black hair hanging down behind her chair.

"It is nice to have company," Cassandra said. "Not many people come to see me. They think I'm sort of crazy, living here by myself all year long. But I like it."

Suddenly remembering what Mrs. Buckley once said, Marilyn blurted out, "Mother didn't mean what she said about . . . about your being a witch."

Cassandra smiled. "It's hard for people to understand why I live like this. Sometimes I even wonder about it myself."

"Do you even like it in winter, too?" Marilyn asked.

"Yes. The ocean is very different in the winter. It almost seems lonely." She laughed. "Sometimes I imagine I am keeping it company."

"But don't you ever get lonely for people, too?"

Cassandra idly picked the crumbs off the table. "That's a question that hurts," she said. "I tell myself I don't, but I think sometimes I do. Maybe that's why I always look forward to summer. I like having people around, even though they don't come to see me."

"I'd be lonely," Marilyn said earnestly. "I feel lonely even when my whole family is around, because there isn't anybody really special."

"Nobody special?" asked Cassandra. "Aren't your parents and your brothers special?"

"But nobody likes me best of all."

Cassandra frowned thoughtfully. "It's strange. What you want is what I've been most afraid of. I guess I've always been afraid that if I found somebody who liked me more than anybody else, I would have to give up too many things I like to do, like wading in the ocean or picking up driftwood or sitting by myself under the stars."

It *was* strange. Marilyn felt she had been knocking herself out to get Nico to like her especially well. And meanwhile Cassandra was living like a hermit so she

69

wouldn't have to be special to anybody.

"Well," said Cassandra, lifting her long hair to cool her neck. "Perhaps we are both a little bit right and a little bit wrong. Perhaps, if you ever find that special friend of yours, you will wish you were not quite so special after all. And perhaps . . . if . . . someone ever finds me . . . way out here on the beach . . . I'll wish he had found me sooner."

An hour had gone by before Marilyn realized it.

"Please come again, Marilyn," Cassandra said. "It's been fun talking with you—really."

"Maybe you could have dinner with us some evening," Marilyn suggested.

Cassandra's eyes twinkled merrily. "I will wait until your mother invites me—when she is quite sure I am not a witch."

By the tenth of July, the workmen had finished the repairs on the boarding house, and Father had just hung up the big "Cliff House" sign when the Pennsylvania art colony arrived. There were five women and three men, and they all wore slacks and sunglasses like everybody else. Marilyn wouldn't have known they were artists if they hadn't carried sketch pads with them.

She liked Ward Evans best. He was a young man of thirty-two with a brush haircut who went around in a T-shirt and looked as though he were going out to play golf. But he liked to paint pictures of "beach people," as he called them. He painted old fat women wrapped in raincoats; grizzled men fishing off the pier; pretty girls splashing in the water; and small children digging wells in the sand. Sometimes, after supper, he got one of the children to pose for him, and Marilyn was delighted when she saw herself on canvas.

But Mother wouldn't let him paint Ricky.

7

The Golden Octopus

Saturday was Mrs. Buckley's birthday. Out on the front porch, the children counted their money.

"Twenty-nine cents," said Peter, emptying his pockets.

"I've got two dimes and Danny has a nickel," said Marilyn.

Nico opened his change purse. "One dime, two nickels, and two pennies," he said. "And these. . . ."

"What are they?" Marilyn asked, looking at the coins in his hand. "Is that Greek money?"

Nico nodded. "Each is called a *drachma*. But I cannot spend them in America. They are like a . . . remembrance of my country."

They walked down the boardwalk looking in the shop windows. They almost bought a white glass sea gull, but Marilyn shook her head. "Mother really wanted something big for a living room decoration. I wish we could buy a big mirror or a stuffed fish or something."

Nico swooped down and picked up Danny, setting him on his shoulders. "We could have Danny stuffed," he suggested playfully. "We could pin him up there above the fireplace by his ears."

Danny howled gleefully and pulled at Nico's hair. "How would I eat if I was stuck up on the wall?" he asked.

"You would not need food," Nico said, his eyes smiling. "You would be stuffed—you would be full all the time. Then we would not have to put an ice cream cone in you every afternoon."

Farther on, a crowd had gathered at the door of the auction shop. The children squeezed through. Up in front, surrounded by trunks and teapots, the auctioneer spoke rapidly as though he were holding his breath.

"Here I have ladies and gentlemen a silver service owned by one of the finest first families of Virginia. What am I bid ladies and gentlemen and don't embarrass yourselves by starting too low. Only the most unusual circumstances placed this silver in my hands and it is worthy of a place in any museum. What do I hear now what do I hear? Fifteen dollars you must be joking, sir.

Twenty? Twenty-five over here twenty-eight do I hear thirty? Forty dollars forty-five dollars for this beautiful set ladies and gentlemen who'll make it fifty? Fifty-five dollars do I hear sixty? Fifty-five dollars who'll make it sixty? You, sir? Don't raise your hand if you're not bidding, sir. Fifty-five once. . . . fifty-five twice. . . . *sold* to the man in the straw hat for fifty-five dollars!"

Peter found seats in the first row, and the children sat wide-eyed.

Next to go up for sale was a big rose-colored lamp.

"Oh, I wish we could get that for Mother!" Marilyn breathed, but the bidding began at six dollars.

After the lamp there was a bicycle and a necklace and a set of golf clubs. Then the auctioneer opened a big box beside him and laughed.

"Now, ladies and gentlemen, the catch of the year! I guarantee that none of you have ever seen the likes of what is in this box."

He reached down and pulled out a huge papier-maché octopus, painted gold, with big black eyes that looked sideways and eight long tentacles that turned up. Everyone laughed.

"A left-over from last year's carnival," the auctioneer said. "I don't know how it got in here, but let's see who the lucky person will be."

No one bid.

"Don't tell me no one wants a golden octopus," said the silver-haired man up in front. "Why, you could put it on your patio or in your bathtub or put it over your

head on Halloween."

"Mother could hang it in the living room!" Marilyn whispered excitedly to Peter.

The auctioneer looked down at the children. "What about you? What am I bid for this fine gold friend?"

"Five cents," whispered Peter.

"What?"

"Five cents," said Peter, louder.

Everybody laughed.

"Five cents," repeated the auctioneer. "Who'll make it ten?"

"Ten," yelled somebody.

"Fifteen cents," said Peter.

"Fifteen cents," said the auctioneer. "Who'll make it twenty-five? Not everybody can have an octopus in his house, you know."

"Twenty-five," said a lady.

"Fifty," said Peter, getting bolder.

"Sixty," said somebody.

Peter counted the change in his hand. "Seventy-six cents," he said.

"Seventy-six cents! You really want that octopus, boy, don't you?" said the auctioneer.

"It's my mother's birthday," said Peter. "We want it for her."

"Give it to him," somebody yelled.

The auctioneer shook his head. "Nothing goes for less than a dollar. It's the rule. Make it a buck, sonny, and it's yours."

76

"Seventy-six cents is all we've got," said Peter.

Nico got up and walked toward the auctioneer. "Would you take these, mister?" he asked timidly, holding out the Greek coins.

The auctioneer looked down and frowned. "Huh? What's this? Spic money, huh?" He turned to the audience. "The Greek kid here gave me a couple coins. Somebody give me twenty-four cents for the spic money and I'll let the kids take the octopus."

"Here," said someone, holding out the change, and the silver-haired man handed the big box to Nico and Peter.

Outside, Marilyn was jubilant and hugged Nico's arm. "If it wasn't for you, we couldn't have bought it," she said. "Did you really mind giving up the coins, Nico?"

Nico's eyes flashed. "I did not mind the giving up so much as I mind the names. Spic money! The man has no heart. I am glad he himself did not get them. He would bend them and scratch them and think they should sing."

Peter looked surprised at this outburst. "I guess he's never been to Greece, Nico. He doesn't know anything about the country or the people or the money. . . ."

"He should *not* come, either," Nico declared vehemently. "The rocks would jump up and strike his ankles."

Danny stared. "Really, Nico?"

Suddenly the dark-haired boy laughed. He picked up a rock and threw it as hard as he could, way out over

77

the beach to the water's edge. "No," he said. "Only people throw stones. Only people call each other names."

At supper that evening, Mrs. Buckley served a chocolate cake she had made. Julius and Miss Tugberry gave her a box of candy, and Father gave her a pink blouse. Ward surprised everyone by presenting her with a portrait of Danny. There were tears in Mother's eyes as she thanked him.

"You do beautiful work," she said. "Some day you will be great and famous."

Ward smiled as he forked into his cake. "*Some* day! My dear Mrs. Buckley, don't you know that you are already harboring one of the world's greatest artists under your roof?" Everybody laughed and Ward added, "Some day, long after this house is gone, someone will find this portrait buried in the sand, and he will scrape away the layers of dust and mud and say, 'Look! An original portrait by Ward Evans,' and your son Danny will be hung in the great art galleries of the world."

Danny squirmed. "I don't want to hang up anywhere. And I don't want my throat stuffed, either."

"What in the world is he talking about?" asked Mrs. Buckley, but Marilyn and Peter and Nico were laughing so hard they couldn't answer.

It was time to open the big box. The children had drawn flowers all over it with crayons. Nico had drawn donkeys.

"What is it, Ralph?" Mother asked.

Father shrugged. "They wouldn't tell me. A hat, maybe?"

The children giggled.

"No, it's not," yelled Danny. "It's a. . . . ."

Three pairs of hands clapped quickly over his mouth, and Danny blushed.

Mother opened the lid and reached inside. A second later the big gold octopus with the eyes that turned sideways and the tentacles that curled upwards was hoisted out of the box. Miss Tugberry gasped.

"It's an . . . an. . . ." Mother just stared without finishing.

"Octopus!" said Father, his eyes wide. "Well, I'll be!"

"For the love of Mike!" said Ward.

Julius threw back his head and laughed. "A golden one at that!"

"Wh . . . what shall I do with it?" Mother asked the four grinning children.

"It's for the living room," Marilyn burbled. "You said you wanted something that looked like it came from the ocean."

Mother gulped. "Well . . . I . . . of course!" She took a deep breath and glanced at Father. "Where shall I hang it?"

The space above the piano seemed just right. No matter where they sat in the big living room they could see it. Every time someone opened the front door, the wind caught the big gold thing and turned it slowly this way and that.

79

The children stood and admired it. Later, when the other artists came back from a movie in town, they said it added a touch of whimsy to Cliff House, and Mother looked really pleased.

Her parents were sitting on the back porch when Marilyn came out to shake the sand from her shoes. As she leaned over the railing she said, "Daddy, what's spic?"

"You mean—spic and span?"

"No. When people talk about Nico . . ."

Mrs. Buckley stiffened. "Who, Marilyn?"

"The auctioneer. Nico gave him all his Greek coins to help buy your present, and the man said it was spic money."

"Ralph, I'm going to see that man! I won't have anyone calling Nico names. . . ."

"Easy, Pat," said Father. "It's probably not the first time Nico has heard that word and it won't be the last."

"Is it a bad word?" asked Marilyn.

"No. It's a foolish word used by foolish people. You remember the names people called that Negro family who moved into our neighborhood back in Wheaton? Some people hate other people for no other reason than that they were born in another country or have a different color skin or brush their teeth backwards or some other idiotic thing. They don't even bother to get to know them. If they didn't hate Negroes or Greeks, they'd find somebody else to look down on, because the smaller they can make everybody else seem, the taller it makes them feel. Pretty dumb, isn't it?"

80

"Why *not* talk to the auctioneer?" Mother asked.

"It's Nico's battle, honey. We weren't even there. He'll have to learn that Americans—like everyone else—can be foolish at times. But he has to learn to handle these things himself."

And Nico, sitting down under the back porch stroking Sylvia's sleek white throat, listened silently.

8

The Forever Baby

Mr. Buckley stood on the front porch, yelling "Nico! Peter!" He waved at them to come in. The two boys wiped the ocean from their eyes and stood up.

They waded up on the beach and picked up their towels, the hot July sun burning their backs and shoulders. When they reached the house, they saw that Father was wearing a suit and tie. But he still had his beard.

"Where are you going, Dad?" asked Peter.

"Don't you remember? This is the day Mother and I take Ricky to Baltimore. You kids promised to take care of the house."

The boys dressed quickly.

Mother came out of the kitchen. She had on a pretty green dress and a white necklace. "Marilyn's fixing lunch today," she told them, and turning to Danny, she added, "You do as they say, now."

"Why can't I come, too?" Danny scowled. "Every time somebody goes to Bal-le-more I have to stay home."

"I told you, dear. Ricky's going to the doctor and there would be nothing at all for you to do."

"Is he going to get needles stuck in him?"

"No. Just a check-up."

Marilyn, sitting on the couch with Ricky, looked carefully at his little face. He had two arms and two legs, yet something about him was different from other babies. If Mother wouldn't tell her anything when they got back from Baltimore, she would ask Father.

Marilyn busied herself with the breakfast dishes while Danny sat on the counter blowing soap bubbles. The artists came down for their morning coffee and rolls and went out across the sand with their easels.

Nico was picking out a tune on the piano and Peter was thumbing through a travel folder when Julius came downstairs.

"Mr. Buckley around?" Marilyn heard him ask.

"No, he's gone for the day," Peter answered.

"All day, huh?" Julius walked over to the window and looked out. Marilyn saw Nico turn around and roll his eyes at Peter. "Thought maybe he'd loan me a shovel," Julius continued.

83

"Uh . . . uh . . . I think there's one under the back porch," Peter stammered, wide-eyed. "I'll go see."

"No. Don't bother. I'll get it," said Julius, and went out.

"Peter!" gasped Nico. "He is going to do digging!"

Peter stared blankly at Nico. "I'll bet he heard Dad say he was going to Baltimore. I'll bet he knew all along we'd be alone today."

I wish Ward was here, thought Marilyn. He'd know what to do.

The boys ran to the window. Julius was walking across the front yard. He went all the way around the cliff until he came to the beach below.

The boys crept outside and lay flat at the edge of the yard where they could watch, just as they had done before.

All right, Marilyn said to herself. You watch Julius and I'll watch all of you. She went upstairs and watched out a front window.

Julius was obviously looking for the stump. But the hurricane had changed the whole beach. The water came in close now where it used to be far out, and swung far out where it used to be close.

Julius pushed his hat back on his head and started to dig. He took up four shovelfuls of sand and stopped. Then he moved away a few feet and dug again. Around and around he moved, but found nothing. He got down and felt around with his hands. Nothing.

After half an hour, he came back toward the house. Peter and Nico crawled backwards on the ground until they were out of sight of Julius. They just managed to tumble up the steps and inside the door as Julius came around the cliff. Marilyn giggled to herself. The great detectives!

About four o'clock, Miss Tugberry came in for her tea.

"Isn't your mother home yet?" she asked, as Marilyn poured hot water in her china cup. "What doctor did they go to see?"

"I don't know—someone in Baltimore," Marilyn told her.

"Baltimore?" said Miss Tugberry. "That's a long way to go, isn't it?"

Just then they heard a car door close in the alley.

"They're back," said Nico, going to the window.

The back screen opened and Mother came in. Her eyes were red, and her lips trembled. She hurried on through the kitchen to the bedroom and shut the door. When Mr. Buckley came in, Danny said, "Daddy, Mommy was crying."

"I know she was," said Father. He said hello to Miss Tugberry and then, to the children, "Let's go for a walk, kids—down to the pier, and I'll tell you about our trip to Baltimore."

As soon as they were out on the beach, Marilyn slipped her hand in her father's. "Was Mother crying about Ricky?" she asked.

"Yes." Mr. Buckley put his other arm around Nico, and Danny and Peter walked along beside them. "We got some bad news about little Ricky today. For a long time, Mother and I have been worried about him. He doesn't play with toys the way you other children did. He doesn't seem to recognize members of our family— he doesn't try to turn over or sit up—things like that. So we took him to a special doctor in Baltimore to find out if Ricky is okay. And he's not."

"Is he going to have an operation?" Peter asked.

"I wish he could. I wish an operation would make him better. The bad news is that Ricky will never be quite like other children and there's nothing we can do. The doctors call this kind of baby mentally retarded."

"Will he ever walk or talk?" Nico asked.

"The doctor says he'll walk, and talk a little. But he will probably never get a job when he grows up or go to college or get married. . . ."

"Oh, Daddy!" Marilyn said. "He'll just be . . . he'll be a baby forever! He'll grow big like a man but he'll be a baby inside?"

"That's about how it is," said Father. "But we're all going to think about the things Ricky can do instead of the things he can't. And we'll have to help Mother think that way, too. She's awfully upset."

After supper that evening, as Marilyn held Ricky in her arms, she looked down into his blue eyes. His little bobbing head rested against her cheek and he made cooing sounds in his throat.

She tried to think about the things he could enjoy— this forever baby in her arms. He still liked to be loved

and cuddled. He still liked the strawberry ice cream she fed him with a spoon. He still liked to lie outside in his carriage, even though he did not seem to notice the sea gulls flapping about overhead or the soft billowy clouds in the sky. And somehow Marilyn knew that she loved the forever baby even more because he needed it more, and she hugged him close.

9

On Stage

Marilyn and Peter and Nico were sitting on the front steps watching a sailboat on the ocean. The radio in the living room was playing, and suddenly Nico jumped down into the yard. With his arms straight out, he took two steps forward and leaped to one side, two steps back and leaped to the other.

Marilyn and Peter started to clap in time with the music, but Nico stopped, embarrassed.

"It is the music," he grinned. "It is music for *scherza*. It is hard for a Greek not to dance when he hears it."

"Oh, *please* dance some more," Marilyn cried.

"Go on, Nico," said Peter.

The music grew louder and the beat lured him. With his eyes closed, his arms out again, Nico whirled about the yard.

"I didn't know you could dance," said Peter when the music stopped.

Nico laughed. "All Greeks know how to dance. Who can find an American who does not like baseball? In Greece, there is no one who does not like the dance."

Marilyn's eyes were suddenly wide and sparkly. "Let's put on a show!" she cried. "Oh, Nico, I've got a wonderful idea!"

"No, no," said Nico. "I do not like to be made a show of."

"Not just you," Marilyn explained. "All of us. We'll all do something. You could dance, Nico, and Peter could be a magician, and I could do a pantomime. . . ."

Peter began to get interested. "We could use the front porch as a stage and we'd advertise it on the board-walk and everybody would come and we'd have lemonade. Hey, let's do it! Let's put on a big show and charge a quarter to see it! What do you say, Nico?"

Nico laughed. "If everybody else plays the fool, I do it, too."

"What are you gonna play?" asked Danny, from the doorway, pressing his nose flat against the screen. "I wanna play too."

"Danny could be in it!" said Marilyn. "We're going

90

to put on a big show, Danny, and people will pay to see it. What do you want to do in it?"

Danny thought for a moment. "I will ride Sylvia with my bathing suit on," he said, and the others thought that would be perfect.

Father said the idea was great, and he promised to put a rope across the porch for the stage curtain. But it was hard to get Mother to talk. She walked about unsmiling with her eyes sad and red.

"Could we have some old sheets for the curtains, Mother?" Marilyn asked.

"You know where we keep them," Mother said, her lips scarcely moving.

Marilyn sat moodily on a kitchen chair, watching her mother. She felt so lonely inside that she wanted to cry. Before, Mother would have said, "Of course! Let's do it." Now she looked as though she wanted to cry, too.

"Mother, I'm sorry about Ricky," Marilyn began.

"I know," Mrs. Buckley said, swallowing. "But it hurts so to talk about it. Please go do something else, Marilyn."

Marilyn stayed in the chair, tears welling up in her eyes. Mother would never again be the very special friend she'd once been. There were too many other children in the family now to worry about.

"It gets so lonely . . . with nobody to talk to," Marilyn began again, but this time Mrs. Buckley turned quickly around, her eyes red and angry.

"Marilyn, *will* you go do something? *Please?* All I

want is to be left alone."

Marilyn went up to her room and lay down on the bed. She felt she hated Ricky and Nico and Danny and Peter. She wished she'd been born into a family where she was the only child. How could Mother and Father want to adopt still more children? They couldn't even love the ones they had!

That evening, when Marilyn was feeding Ricky on the back porch, she heard her father say in the kitchen, "He's only one of five children, Pat—precious as he is. You can't sacrifice the others for him. . . ."

Mother's voice was loud and sharp. "They have everything, Ralph . . . and Ricky has nothing. Nothing!"

"That's not true, honey. Right now he's got all your love and the others aren't getting any. All the love in the world won't make Ricky grow up any faster. He's got a lot of family to give him love—not just you."

Mother began to cry, and Marilyn sat numbly in the rocking chair, wishing she weren't there.

"I know . . . ," Mother was saying, "and I don't really want to ruin their summer here . . . I wanted it to be happy for all of us. . . ."

Ricky wailed then and Marilyn held him close. Mother and Father lowered their voices and finally stopped talking altogether. But a little later Mother came out on the back porch and said, "I think sheets might be a little too light for curtains, Marilyn. I have two old blankets that should do. Tomorrow we'll get them out and see if they won't fit."

92

Marilyn jumped up with Ricky in one arm and threw the other one around her mother.

"Oh, Mother," she gulped, hugging her, and Mother embraced both Marilyn and Ricky at once. They didn't say any more. They just stood in the soft summer darkness, loving hard.

The big show was to be Friday night. All week long the children worked on it. Nico and Peter tacked posters on the boardwalk that read, "Big show Friday night— 7:00 p.m.—Cliff House, off north end of boardwalk. Stunts—popcorn—lemonade. Everybody come. 25¢."

"Having a big show, huh?" asked Ward, watching them hang the stage curtains. "What are you going to do with all the money you make?"

"Why, give it to Daddy, of course," said Marilyn. "If we don't run out of money, we get to come back again next year."

"I see." Ward rubbed his big chin. "Well, now, how would you like me to sketch portraits for you? I'll charge a dollar maybe, and you can keep the money."

Four happy kids leaped gratefully on him, and Ward yelled, "Hey, if you break my arm, the deal's off."

After that, everybody got in the act. Julius promised to play his harmonica and Miss Tugberry said she would be a fortune teller.

Sometimes shopkeepers gave the children boxes of bubble gum or balloons to sell at their show. And sometimes, the surf boys jeered at them from their hangout in front of the arcade, their bleached hair white under the neon lights.

"Hey, there's the Greek and the carrot tops," one of them would yell. Or, "Hey, greaseball, how's the olive business?"

"What if they come?" Marilyn said to Peter.

"They wouldn't try anything with Dad around," Peter declared.

The big day arrived, warm and sunny. Peter and Nico put rocking chairs out in the yard for the grownups to sit in. The boys and girls could sit on the ground. Marilyn and her mother worked in the kitchen making popcorn and lemonade, and Miss Tugberry made a batch of fudge, which was half gone by evening.

At six o'clock the children were too excited to eat dinner. At six-thirty Danny had a stomach ache, Marilyn stubbed her toe, and Peter and Nico spilled a jar of lemonade. But by seven, the jitters were gone. Twenty-nine children sat in front of the house where Ward was collecting quarters, and there were grown-ups too. In-side the house, Miss Tugberry put on an old record, "Alexander's Ragtime Band," and the curtain opened with a shower of balloons. Danny came out in his red bathing trunks, riding on Sylvia's back. The children clapped and cheered.

All week long they had practiced it. Every day Peter put Danny on Sylvia's back and led her around the porch. Each time, Sylvia did her part well, prancing around and smiling her silly goat smile.

94

But they had not practiced with the balloons or the clapping, and Sylvia jerked her head nervously as the children yelled, skidding to the right and then to the left. Suddenly her hoof came down on a balloon. Bang! The goat leaped up in the air, her four legs flying out at all angles. Danny fell off one side. His feet hit the porch and he tumbled backwards in a perfect somersault, landing on his feet, while Sylvia went flying off the porch, over the heads of the children in the front row.

The audience whooped. Ward, who was standing off to one side, made a dive for Sylvia, missed, and fell flat on his stomach with a loud *oof!* Off Sylvia ran across the yard and around the house, where she clattered up on the back porch and maa-ed disgustedly.

Danny bowed and hurried into the house, his lips trembling. Mrs. Buckley grabbed him in her arms, laughing now that the scare was over.

"You were a real hit, honey! The children loved it!"

"I don't wanna do that any more," Danny wept.

Mother hugged him. "I wouldn't let you do it again in a thousand years."

Peter was on stage now. He wore a tall black cardboard hat. He did the disappearing money act and the handkerchief act, and turned a deck of black playing cards into red ones. When he was all done, he took off his hat, and out tumbled a dozen pieces of bubblegum which he threw to the audience. The children clapped hard.

"It's going great!" Father said, as Peter came in.

Among the audience, however, were some who were not welcome. The surf boys crawled up the cliff, and watched Danny and Peter with amusement. When Marilyn went on, they made her nervous.

She wore a long blue skirt of Mother's and a pretty blouse. Miss Tugberry had made a little crown of white roses for Marilyn to wear in her hair.

"I'm going to tell you a story," Marilyn began, "but it will not be in words. It is a story you all know—*Cinderella*."

Marilyn began as Cinderella scrubbing the floor, wearily going about her chores, and alternately became the haughty stepsisters and stepmother.

By moving her arms and her body, Marilyn showed the pumpkin being turned into a carriage and the mice into horses. At the end, when she portrayed the prince trying the slipper on the feet of the stepsisters, the small children in the first row shouted, "Try Cinderella! Try Cinderella!"

The audience seemed to like it, but now and then a ripple of laughter from the edge of the cliff made her flush. Once she tripped over her dress and the laughter of the surf boys was loud and raucous.

The audience clapped when Marilyn was through, but she knew she could have done better. Mostly, however, she worried about Nico. What would the surf boys do when *he* went on?

Julius was next. He pulled out his harmonica and started in with "Oh, Susannah." By the time he got to the end, the audience was singing with him, and after he did "Camp Town Ladies" and "Home on the Range," the adults were clapping their hands.

Nico was last. In a plain white shirt and dark trousers, he came out on the stage. He waited a moment for the music to begin and then, holding his arms straight out at his sides, began the little steps and leaps that made up the Greek dance.

The surf boys grew bolder. They had hooted a little at Peter and laughed at Marilyn and nothing happened. Now, as Nico began a dance they did not understand, their jeers carried distinctly to the stage.

Marilyn went around the yard to Ward.

"Can you make them stop?" she begged. "They'll ruin it."

"I thought they were friends of Nico's," Ward told her. "I saw him surfing with them the other day."

Marilyn stared up at him. "*Nico?* With *them?* Are you sure?"

"Positive. I stopped and talked with him."

"Well, they don't sound like friends," Marilyn said, puzzled. "And they're ruining it for everybody else."

Ward walked around behind the audience to the cliff.

"Okay, you guys, knock it off," he said.

"We can watch, can't we?" said one of the surf boys snidely.

"If you want to watch, pay your money and come on up in the yard like everybody else," Ward told them.

"You own the beach?" said one of the boys.

Ward moved closer. "I said pay up or clear out," he repeated, his big shoulders rising. "You're lousing up the show."

The surf boys surveyed Ward for a minute, and Marilyn wasn't sure whether they were going to jump him or leave.

"C'mon," one of them said finally. "Let's blow. Who wants to see pretty boy up there?"

They slid back down to the beach, and Marilyn turned to watch Nico.

He had his eyes closed now, and though his body seemed to move slowly, his feet were going faster. Now he was turning around and around, faster and faster.

The adults began to clap in time to the music. Then the boys and girls took it up and finally the grown-ups were standing up so they could see better. When the record stopped and Nico made his bow, the audience cheered and cheered.

"More! More! Dance some more!" they yelled, and Mrs. Buckley whispered, "Go ahead, Nico. Dance again."

Nico smiled a little as the music started again. But this time he jerked a white handkerchief from his pocket and waved it around in the air as he danced, as they do in Greece.

A nickel hit the stage, then a couple of pennies and a dime. More and more pennies came flying through the air. Nico's face was flushed and his shirt was damp from dancing, but still his feet flew. At the end, as the record stopped, he leaned breathlessly against the house, gasping and holding his sides as the people yelled, "More! More! More!"

Nico started to speak but no one could hear him. Then, as someone cried, "Shhhhhhh," the audience quieted down and Nico panted, "I wish . . . I had . . . four legs . . . so that two could dance for you . . . while the others rested. . . ." The people laughed. "But I have only two, and they are tired, so I must stop. I thank you." And he went inside.

The show was over and it had been a success. Peter and Nico picked up all the money on the stage while Marilyn and Mrs. Buckley passed out popcorn and lemonade in paper cups. A crowd gathered around Ward, who was sketching a little girl for a dollar. Down under the house, in the curtained shower stall, Miss Tugberry sat with a fancy shawl around her shoulders, big gold earrings dangling from her ears, and bracelets all up and down her wrinkled arms.

By the light of a little red lamp, she told fortunes for a nickel, and Marilyn and Peter and Nico stood outside, giggling as she talked of stars and fates and tea leaves to the wide-eyed children who tiptoed in.

"Get Julius," Peter whispered to Marilyn. "Let's see what she says about him, just for fun."

"My fortune?" smiled Julius. "Well, that ought to be interesting. For a nickel, how can I lose? You wait till Ward here finishes drawing this ugly mug of mine, and I'll give it a try."

When Miss Tugberry saw him coming, she pulled aside the curtain and stuck her head out. "Ah, come in, my good man, and let me look at the lines the years have made on you," she said, her eyes laughing.

Julius laughed too and sat down at the little table across from her while the three children gathered around the door. Miss Tugberry took Julius' hand and frowned thoughtfully at the lines on the palm.

"Ah . . . I see it . . . I see something here . . . something deep and dark and mysterious. . . ."

"What . . . what is it?" Marilyn whispered.

"Shhhh . . . do not break the spell," said Miss Tugberry. "I cannot tell what it is. . . ."

"Let me try," said another voice.

The children turned to see Cassandra standing behind them. Miss Tugberry and Julius stared too, for in the eerie light of the candle, Cassandra's sun-browned skin seemed to glisten like the little earrings in her ears, and her white teeth sparkled as she smiled.

"Let me try to read his fortune," she said. "The stars and I are old friends." She sat down on the floor in front of Julius. "Give me your hand, Mr. Green, and let me see if they talk to us tonight."

Julius slowly held out his hand while Miss Tugberry and the children crowded around.

"You were right, Miss Tugberry," said Cassandra, looking at Julius' hand. "There is something mysterious here . . . something buried . . . something of the present and something of the past. . ."

101

Julius pulled his hand away and got up. "That's all, ladies," he said, managing a faint smile. "No more, no more. You've gone too far already."

He brushed past them and went outside. Marilyn's heart was in her mouth. Cassandra *had* seen something. Had Miss Tugberry seen it, too? In the eerie light of the candle, both women looked like witches.

It was after nine o'clock when the last child went home. The young Buckleys sprawled on the living room rug and counted the money in the glass jar. Ward gave them the six dollars he had received for his sketches, and Miss Tugberry had made a dollar fifteen.

Marilyn and Nico arranged the silver in piles, and Peter counted it. When he had finished he could hardly believe it.

"Twenty-one dollars and seventeen cents!" he cried.

"You did a real business!" said Mr. Buckley, surprised. "What in the world are you going to do with all that money?"

Marilyn looked at him. "Why . . . it's for Cliff House, so we can come back next year. What did you think?"

Father's mouth dropped open. "Pat, did you know they were going to do this?"

Mother shook her head. "No, but I think they're wonderful! I've got four—five of the most wonderful children that ever lived."

"Well, we can certainly use it," said Father. "It will help make next month's payment on the house. But I

102

won't take it all. I want each of you kids to keep a dollar and buy something for yourselves—something to help you remember Cliff House when we go back to Wheaton."

"I'm going to save mine until I get enough for a shell bracelet," Marilyn decided.

"I know how I'm going to spend mine but I'm not going to tell," said Peter. "You wait and see."

There was a scream from the back porch. Mr. Buckley leaped up.

"It sounds like Miss Tugberry," said Mother.

Everyone raced through the kitchen and out back. Miss Tugberry was leaning against the porch railing, her eyes wide in the shadows. There stood Sylvia, the goat, with all her long, white beautiful hair cut off. Only spotty patches remained, and the floor was littered with the silky stuff while Sylvia stood skinny and pink and shivering against the wall.

"What in the world?" said Father. "Who did this?"

Miss Tugberry could only gasp.

"Oh, this is terrible!" said Mother. "Why, I didn't hear a sound! Why would anybody do a thing like that?"

Miss Tugberry began to cry, and Father helped her sit down.

"It was a horrible thing to do, Miss Tugberry," he said, "and I'll certainly tell the police about it. I just can't imagine who would do it."

"All . . . all her beautiful hair," Miss Tugberry wept. "It will take months to grow back again. . . ."

As Marilyn swept up the goat's hair, she wondered about the boarding house. What strange things went on here—the thing they had seen in the front yard the first night they arrived; the tapping in the wall; Julius burying things in the sand; and now a goat with no hair. What would happen next?

As she went to bed that night, she passed by Ward's room at the back. The light was on and the door was half open.

Ward was still dressed. He was sitting by his easel, absorbed in a picture he was painting. He seemed to be painting over a sketch he had made of somebody that evening. Marilyn stopped and squinted through the door. Her eyes grew wide. It was a portrait of Cassandra. And under Ward's brush, she looked almost beautiful.

10

Secret in the Sand

Peter bought a pigeon. He got it from a man who strolled the boardwalk with a big wicker basket of birds on his back.

"This is a special pigeon," the man told him, "a homing pigeon. You can train her to fly to your house. Every day, take her a little farther away and let her go. She will learn to fly home. But do not let her loose when there are flocks of other birds around, or she may decide to join them."

The Buckleys loved her. White, with a gray-brown

breast and tail feathers, she soared gracefully around the living room and daintily pecked at the cornmeal the children gave her.

For the next few weeks, Peter worked with her constantly, and Nico often helped. Each morning Peter took her down the beach and let her go. Each time, she flew high up in the air and circled around. Then, when she got her bearings, she came down lower and flew straight back to Cliff House where Nico rewarded her with a snail or a worm. Sometimes the boys taped a message to her leg, and the pigeon always came back with it.

Marilyn watched all this silently. Peter knew she would have loved to help train the bird. But it seemed that the more eager she was to share in what he did, the less he wanted her.

Nico, however, was not always around when Peter wanted him. What Ward had said about Nico surfing with the boys down the beach was true, and now he made no secret of it. Several mornings a week he took the surf board Father had bought him and went out to find them.

"I don't understand that boy, Pat," Marilyn over-heard her father say to her mother one morning. "From what Peter tells me, those boys rarely talk to Nico without insulting him. Yet he pals around with them and they let him. It doesn't make sense."

"Maybe it's because he's so good at surfing. Perhaps he just likes to show off," Mother said.

Meanwhile, the police couldn't do anything about

poor Sylvia. There had been too many people there that night, they said, to pin the blame on anybody in particular.

One morning Marilyn lay on the beach looking up at the clouds through her sunglasses and digging her toes in the hot sand. Overhead, the gulls screeched and cawed. Marilyn liked to listen to the strange pattern of their calling.

"What do you think they're singing about, Peter?" she asked as he and Nico sat in the sand writing a message to tape on the pigeon's leg.

"Who?"

"The gulls."

Peter laughed impatiently. "What do you mean? That's no song—just screeching."

"It *could* be a song," Marilyn said. "Don't you think so, Nico?"

"Perhaps," said Nico.

Peter grunted. "Well, it isn't. It's not a song like a cardinal or a mockingbird sings. It's just stupid screeching from stupid birds. And if they don't go away, I might lose my pigeon."

But they are singing, Marilyn told herself as she watched the boys go off down the beach. She lay back down and looked up at the sky again where the gulls were circling. She imagined that they were singing about the waves and the fish beneath them and the sand crabs which crawled frantically around at night looking for a place to hide.

But the gulls didn't help the loneliness. Why couldn't Mother and Father have adopted a girl? Why did Peter get Nico too, on top of everything else?

"Everything *what* else?" Father had said when Marilyn once asked him about it.

"Oh, you know." Marilyn had said. "Peter's the smartest—he wins all the prizes. I'll bet sometimes you wish you didn't have me at all."

"There's an ocean of love to go around, Mar," Father had said. "And there's even some left over. If Peter wins prizes, then that's the way it is. But you're smart, too, honey, and there are many wonderful things about you."

"Like what?" Marilyn had asked.

"Like one green eye and one gray one," Father laughed, and gave her a hug.

Mother, too, had tried to explain about Nico. "We really didn't care whether we got a boy or a girl. We just wanted some child who wanted to be adopted, and Nico did. We liked all the things we had heard about him. Not many people, you see, want to adopt a boy his age or a child from another country. Most want a small baby to raise as their own—a baby that looks as much like them as possible. But that leaves so many children left out. Perhaps we'll adopt a girl later. But Nico does not belong to Peter. Nico belongs only to himself."

Now, as she lay there in the sand, Marilyn fantasied that some day something terrible would happen to her. Perhaps she would drown or suffocate in her bed, and then her parents and her brothers would weep and cry and remember how many times she had been left out of things. The more she thought about it, the sadder she grew, and there were even tears in her eyes beneath the sunglasses.

At that moment, her right toe, pushing deep in the sand, touched something cold and smooth. She wriggled her foot. It felt like a bottle. She sat up and dug it up with her hands.

Suddenly she was on her knees, staring at a little glass bottle with a piece of paper rolled up inside. Quickly she unscrewed the top and pulled out the paper.

There were the strangest words she had ever seen: *Sfnfncfs pomz xibu xbt boe gpshfu uif sftu.*

Her eyes grew wide. A secret code! She turned the bottle over. On the front was a sticker which read, "For reward, return to room 209, Cliff House." Julius' room!

She jumped up as Nico and Peter came walking back.

"Got to get more tape. The message fell off," Peter said.

"Look!" Marilyn cried, giving her secret away. "I found the bottle that Julius hid! Look! I found it!"

Before she could say any more, Peter and Nico were crowding around her. Peter grabbed the note.

"What do *you* know about it?" he said. "This is just between Nico and me."

"No, it isn't!" said Marilyn. "I've been watching you and Julius both! I know all about his burying things in the sand."

110

"Oh, no!" Peter said. "She'll ruin everything! She'll go blabbing to everybody."

Marilyn's face flushed hotly. "If you don't let me in on this, I'm going right up to Julius' room and tell him I found that bottle."

Peter groaned. "Okay," he said finally, and unrolled the paper. Marilyn and Nico crowded around him.

"It's some kind of secret code," said Marilyn. "He must want it back awfully bad, because he's offering a reward."

"That's it!" said Peter. "I'll bet a secret agent was supposed to pick it up."

"He wants to destroy the evidence," said Nico. "Now what shall we do?"

By afternoon they had a plan. When Mother took Ricky and Danny to the supermarket and Father was working in the back yard, Marilyn crept into her parents' bedroom to work on her disguise. First she piled her long red hair up high and tucked it under one of Mother's big floppy hats. Next she put on Mother's lipstick and powder and a pair of dark glasses. She tied a pink scarf around her neck, put on a pair of gloves, one of Mother's blouses over her own skirt, and a pair of high-heeled shoes. Then she practiced walking up and down until she could do it gracefully without tripping. When Nico and Peter saw her they could hardly believe it. She looked like a twenty-year-old lady.

"Glahd to meet you, I'm sure," Marilyn said, extending her gloved hand to Nico, who laughed and shook

111

it so hard her glove fell off.

"Boy, he'll never recognize you," said Peter. "And remember, don't say any more than you have to. Just give him the bottle and see how he acts. We'll be right down the hall in case you need us."

"What if he tries to strangle me?" Marilyn said dolefully, peering over the rims of her sunglasses which had slipped down on her nose.

"Yell real loud and we'll come running," Peter promised.

Marilyn tried squeezing her neck and yelling at the same time. "I don't think it would work," she said, turning red in the face.

"Oh, silly, he won't try to *murder* you. Go on before Mother gets home."

With her heart pounding, Marilyn went upstairs to the second floor and walked softly down the hall.

She cleared her throat, pulled the hat down farther on her forehead, and knocked on Julius' door.

"Yes? Who is it?"

Marilyn didn't answer.

"Who is it?" Julius called again. Then he came to the door and looked out. "Hello?"

"Uh . . . room 209?" Marilyn asked hesitantly, trying to lower her voice. "I found a bottle on the beach, sir, and I . . . uh . . . guess you want it back."

Julius looked at her and then at the bottle. "Yes, it's mine," he said, eagerly. "I'm glad to have it back. Please come in and I'll pay you. So you discovered my secret?"

112

Marilyn's knees began to tremble. "Uh . . . I . . . didn't pay any attention to what it said," she stammered.

The man looked at her strangely. "You didn't? Weren't you curious about the odd words on the paper?"

"Yes . . . I mean, no . . . uh . . . I mean, I think I'd better be going. I . . . I don't want any reward . . . really."

"Oh, no you don't," said Julius. "You found that bottle and now. . . ."

There was a shriek from the doorway and a second later Miss Tugberry stuck her head in the room.

"Marilyn! I declare! What in the world have you got on?" she exclaimed, holding up a long lock of red hair that was hanging down Marilyn's back.

"Marilyn?" cried Julius.

At that moment Nico and Peter, hearing the scream, came tumbling into the room and grabbed Marilyn.

"Don't you try to hurt our sister!" said Peter.

Julius sank down on the bed. "What in the world is going on?" he moaned.

"If you are a spy, we shall call the police, so do not try to leave," said Nico.

Julius gasped. "A spy! It's Marilyn who's going around dressed like Mata Hari, not me!"

Miss Tugberry took off Marilyn's hat and glasses. "My dear, what on earth are you playing?" she asked.

But Peter said, "Come clean, Julius. What's it all about? We saw you bury that bottle at night. And don't try to destroy the evidence. We've already copied down the message."

113

Julius stared at Peter. Suddenly he threw back his head and laughed—a big laugh like a horse showing all its teeth.

"So that's it, eh? You found my bottle and now I'm a spy! Well, well. I had no idea it was going to turn into all this."

"Julius Green," said Miss Tugberry. "What in the world is all this about?"

"Everybody sit down," said Julius. "I will tell you my story. Then if you want to call the police I shall go willingly. I shall even put on the handcuffs myself."

The children sat down. In fact, Marilyn fell down because she stumbled in Mother's big shoes.

"That's better," said Julius. "Now you do not look like constables come to carry me off." He walked over to the side window and stood looking out over the boardwalk in the distance. "I never thought I'd be telling this story to anyone—or that there was any story left to tell." He turned around and said to Peter and Nico, "It's a love story. Are you sure you want to hear it?"

"Awk!" said Peter.

"Oh, yes, please," Marilyn begged.

"Well, thirty-three years ago, when I was a young man, I came to the ocean to spend the summer. I got a job as a lifeguard about where the pier is now. That summer, I met the loveliest girl I had ever seen. She had skin as white as a lily and hair like a raven's. Every day she came down to the beach with her mother and sat under a big umbrella."

114

Julius sat down on the edge of the bed. "By and by, the girl began coming around by herself, and I knew she liked me as much as I liked her. Her name was Alice. Sometimes after I got off duty I'd walk down the beach with my arm around her and she'd sing. I was . . . was never so happy in my life. But her parents didn't like me, maybe because I hadn't all the schooling Alice had. They forbade Alice to see me anymore, so we began to see each other secretly. I'll bet you can guess where she lived."

"Where?" asked Marilyn.

"Right here."

The children gasped.

"Every time I thought about her, I'd think about this house. I'd wonder what she was doing and what room she was in."

"What ever happened?" asked Miss Tugberry.

"Well, her parents found out that we were still seeing each other, and wouldn't let her go out at night. So we began writing notes to each other. Every day Alice would bury a note in a bottle right beside the old stump. And every night, after dark, I'd come and get the note and leave one of my own. Her parents never guessed.

"Finally, near the end of the summer, we made plans to run off and get married. I was going to take her back home to Buffalo and get a job in a shoe store there, and Alice was going to give music lessons. But the day we were going to elope, her parents found out and whisked her off to another city. I never heard from her again."

115

"Oh, Julius, what a sad story," said Miss Tugberry. "Didn't she leave a note for you?"

"That's what I'd hoped," said Julius. "After she left, I went to the stump, but there was nothing there. I even came back the following summer and got my job as lifeguard again. But she wasn't here. When I left that year, I vowed never to set foot in town again. But . . ." He smiled at the children. "Here I am, thirty-three years later. I needed a vacation and decided to see what the town looked like after all these years. I was surprised to find that this house had been turned into a boarding house. I decided to stay here, wondering if it would bring back all the old feelings I had about her. And it did."

"But what about the bottle and this message?" asked Peter.

Julius picked it up and frowned. "This is really strange. Believe me, but I don't know any more about it than you do. Naturally, after all these years, I was curious to know if any message had ever been left in the years between, and, not expecting to find anything, I dug around the stump one day. You can imagine my surprise when I found a message in the same code that Alice and I had used. But it was not signed by Alice."

"What did it say?" Marilyn breathed.

"It said, *Can you be the same Julius Green? Alice is gone.* I am very puzzled. If Alice is gone, who else knew about our hiding place and our code? And who in the world besides Alice would ever recognize me after all these years?"

116

"Heavens above!" cried Miss Tugberry. "This is better than a movie!"

Julius opened the bottle that Marilyn had brought him. "When I found that first message, I immediately wrote one myself. I begged the person to tell me who he was and what had become of Alice. It seemed that one of you kids was always about, and I did not know who else might be watching, so I went out late one night and hid it in the same old place beside the stump. For days I watched to see who would come and pick it up, but I saw no one. Then finally, a few days later, I checked and the note was gone. Someone must have come in the night. I was hoping he would come back again and leave another note, but the hurricane came instead and buried the stump."

He unfolded the paper in the bottle and looked at the words. Then he took a pencil from his shirt pocket and jotted down the letters.

"What is the code, Julius?" asked Nico.

"It is very simple, really," Julius smiled. "Look. Here is the first word in the message: *sfnfncfs*. Now, all I have to do is write down the letters that come before each of these letters in the alphabet. See? What comes before 's'?"

"R," said Peter. Julius wrote it down.

"Now what comes before 'f'?"

"E," said Marilyn.

Julius continued with all the letters until he got the word, *Remember*. Then he did the same with the other

117

words. He silently read the message, then handed it to Miss Tugberry.

"Remember only what was and forget the rest," she read slowly.

Julius threw up his hands. "How can I? After thirty-three years, I find a message like this! Why, I'll go crazy if I don't find out." He jumped up suddenly. "Show me the exact place you found the bottle," he said. "If I can find the stump again and uncover it, perhaps the person will leave some more messages."

They all hurried outside.

"Uh . . . I think it was right about there . . . somewhere," Marilyn said hesitantly.

"No, over here," said Nico.

"You're both nuts," said Peter. "It was way down there. I'm sure of it."

No one could agree. The more they argued the more they changed their minds, and finally they admitted it could be anywhere on the beach. They had forgotten to notice.

Later, when the children were talking about it, Peter said, "Should we tell Dad?"

"I don't think so," said Nico. "It was a personal secret. It is really none of our business. I think perhaps we should keep this secret for Julius."

One afternoon, Marilyn and Nico went down on the beach to look for shells that had washed up during the night.

"Huh!" Marilyn said. "Peter didn't want me in on

118

that secret about Julius! If it hadn't been for me, he wouldn't have found out anything!"

Nico sifted through a handful of shells, looking for ones that weren't chipped. "I do not understand it," he said at last. "Why do you and Peter fight so much?"

Marilyn sat down beside Nico and dug both bare feet into the sand up to her ankles. Then she wiggled her toes and the sand crumbled over them. "Sometimes I feel that my parents love Peter more than me. He's smarter, you know."

"I did not notice," said Nico. "It is strange that you think that. Because Peter said. . . ." He stopped suddenly . "No, I should not tell these things. . . ."

"Oh, please!" said Marilyn, curious. "What did Peter say?"

"Well, it is funny. He said that you are the family pet because you are the only girl—and that your parents treat you like a big angora cat."

Marilyn and Nico both laughed.

"It *is* funny," said Marilyn. "But it's not true." Suddenly she asked the question she'd been afraid to ask. "Nico, you are going to live with us, aren't you? Always, I mean. . . .?"

Nico sat silently, turning the shells over and over in his hand. "Well, my head is still thinking . . . I have not decided about it. . . . ."

"Don't you like us, Nico?"

"Of course. That is not it at all. But I . . . do not know . . . if I can ever be what you and Peter and Danny

119

are to your parents . . ."

Marilyn stared at him. "But you were chosen, Nico! When I was born to them, they had to take me even if I had three arms and two heads! But when they sent for you, they knew all about you."

Nico stood up and tossed the broken shells, one by one, into the water. "That makes me sound so special. But that is what I do not like."

Marilyn could not understand. Didn't Nico feel that Mother and Father loved him? They gave him just as much hugging as everyone else. Perhaps Nico, like Ricky, needed more. Perhaps that was what was wrong. But that didn't make sense either, because a little later, she saw him out surfing with the boys from the other end of the beach. If it wasn't love Nico needed, what was it?

That night, after Marilyn went to bed, she heard the knocking again. *Tap . . . tap tap tap . . . tap . . . tap tap.*

Somehow she felt very brave. She got out of bed and felt her way across the floor to the wall.

"Who's there?" she called out softly.

There was no reply. The knocking stopped. Then it started up again.

Tap tap . . . tap tap . . . tap. . . .

Sometimes it was fast; sometimes it was slow.

Marilyn put her hands on the wall and moved along, back and forth, feeling over the plaster. At a certain place, she could feel the vibration of the tapping and she pulled her hands away quickly, her heart pounding.

"What . . . what do you want?" she called out. But there was no answer.

She had to tell somebody. She put on her robe and went out in the hall. Maybe the best thing to do was to get Father.

She had just reached the second floor when she saw Julius starting up from the landing.

"Good heavens, Marilyn!" he exclaimed. "What are you doing up?"

"There's a strange noise in my room," Marilyn told him. "Please come up and listen. It's in the wall. I think somebody's in there!"

"Somebody in your *wall*!" Julius gasped. "Now, Marilyn, be sensible. . . ."

"Please come up and listen," Marilyn said, so Julius followed her.

Just as she'd feared, the noise had stopped. Marilyn turned on the light.

"It was right here, right in this wall. I've heard it before," Marilyn said, showing him the spot.

Julius knocked lightly along the wall. "The wall's hollow, but so are most walls. If you ever hear it in the daytime, let me know and we'll give it a thorough search. Okay?"

"Okay," said Marilyn glumly. Perhaps the knock wouldn't come anymore. Perhaps she would go back to Wheaton never knowing what it was. If only Julius could have heard it—somebody else besides her. No one would ever believe her.

11

Out to Sea

The air was cool, a little too cool for swimming. Marilyn and Nico and Peter sat on the front steps watching the life guards signaling each other from their high perches all up and down the beach.

Ward came out of the house with his easel and paints.

"Nothing to do?" he asked. "A whole town to explore, and you've got nothing to do?"

"We've been all over the beach," Peter said.

"Uh huh. Just what I thought. All you know is the

beach. C'mon. Let's go for a real walk."

Marilyn jumped up quickly. "Hurry up. Danny's in the house and we can sneak off before he comes. He'd just get tired and have to be carried."

They swarmed around Ward and started off across the sand.

"I wanna go! I wanna go!" Danny yelled inside the house where he had heard Marilyn's remark.

"Get your shoes on first," said Mother. But by the time Danny found them, Ward and the older children were gone.

"Where are we going, Ward?" Peter asked. "The amusement park?"

"Nope."

"The pier?" asked Nico.

"Nope."

"The drugstore?" said Marilyn.

"Ah. It shows how little you've explored since you came here. Well, today I am going to introduce you to your town, if you'll take turns carrying my easel, please," Ward said, and the children had to stretch their legs wide to keep up with him.

They turned off the boardwalk and went down the ramp to the street below. It was like follow-the-leader. Ward led the way. He turned down an alley, climbed up on a barrel, crossed the roof of a shed, and walked up the side stairs of a tourist house and into the third floor entrance with the children at his heels. He walked down the hall, down the inside stairs, said hello to the startled

123

ladies in the lobby, and back out on the sidewalk again while the threesome giggled behind him.

Then, on a back street, they walked until they came to a high board fence, covered with sketches and paintings. Several young men and women were sitting on the sidewalk, waiting for people to come along and buy their pictures.

Ward stopped. "Which painting do you like best?"

The children looked them over.

"The picture of the ballerinas," said Marilyn.

"The ships," said Nico.

"The horses," said Peter.

Ward sighed. "Wouldn't you know? Nobody chose mine."

"Oh, Ward, which one is yours?" asked Marilyn.

Ward showed them the painting he had done of the old man who operated the ferris wheel.

Marilyn made a face. "But he's so ugly! Who wants to hang a picture of an ugly man in the house?"

"Is he?" said Ward. "To me, his wrinkles and dirt and tattered coat are beautiful. That's what makes the man. That's what makes him different from everyone else on the boardwalk."

"But who wants to be different?" Marilyn insisted.

"Ah, ha!" said Ward, wheeling around delightedly. "But you *are* different whether you want to be or not. Everybody is different from everyone else. Those who let it show are the happiest."

"Well, you don't look different from everybody else,"

Peter said. "You don't look like an artist."

"And that's the secret," said Ward, leading them off down the street again. "Some people try very hard not to look different from anybody else. Some people try very hard *to* look different. The really happy person is truly different in the ways he wants to be, and does not have to think up things to do or to wear just to make people stare at him."

"Like the surf boys and their bleached hair," said Marilyn, stealing a look at Nico, but Nico kept his eyes straight ahead.

They poked their heads in an old building where three people were rehearsing a play on the stage.

"Summer stock," said Ward. "Bet you didn't know there was a live theater in town, did you?"

"Get out! Be off!" cried a mustached actor on stage. "You are interrupting the moment!"

Ward saluted in apology and the children tiptoed quietly out again into the bright sunlight.

A huge kettle, twice as big as a bathtub, was boiling outside a seafood restaurant and, as the children watched, a man in a white cap picked up a basket of red, wiggling crabs and dumped them in the pot.

"Ohhhh! How horrible!" Marilyn cried, covering her eyes.

"Only for the crabs," said Ward. "I'm hungry. Let's go next door and get a pizza."

They went inside the Italian restaurant and sat down at a red-checked table.

125

They watched as the cook picked up a ball of dough and tossed it into the air. Again and again he tossed it up, and each time it came down he gave it a punch. Then, working quickly, he spread it out with his fingers until it was as big as a bicycle tire. He covered it with cheese and sausage and mushrooms and put it in the big oven. When it was finally delivered to the table on a big wooden paddle, Ward said, "No forks; fingers only."

They ate—big crusty pieces—with tomato dripping down their chins and hot cheese sticking behind their front teeth.

"Now," said Ward, as he paid the cashier and they went outside again, "I'm afraid our walk is over. You can come up to the dock with me if you want, but then I'm going to work."

Peter had a turn carrying the easel. They walked farther and farther away from the business district. The shops got fewer and, instead of alleys between them, there were now long stretches of sandy fields. They came to a small inlet where the ocean had crept in to rest. There, in the shallow sleepy water, tall weeds waved willowy in the wind and the big white birds stood motionless on one leg. Crickets hopped, and spiders wove monstrous webs from weed to weed.

Finally they came to the dock where grizzled fishermen called to one another, hammering away on their boats and spreading salt-smelly nets out to dry. Ward chose a place and set up his easel.

"Now good-bye," he grinned at the children. "I am

126

not fond of spectators breathing down my neck while I work."

They thanked him for the pizza and ambled on along the dock to watch the fishermen before they started home. The sun was behind the clouds again which seemed to make the wind stronger, and Marilyn was glad she had a jacket.

Suddenly Peter whispered something to Nico. They moved away from Marilyn and whispered some more. Marilyn stopped to wait for them, but Peter said,

"Hey, Mar, you go on home, okay? We've got some business to do."

Marilyn looked at Nico. "It's a long way back," she said. "Can't I come with you?"

Nico shook his head. "We will see you at home," he told her. "This is between Peter and me."

They whispered some more and then ran off down the dock and disappeared behind a packing plant.

Marilyn stood there staring after them. Even Nico was doing it now. Before, she could at least count on a frown from Nico when Peter tried to keep her away, if not an argument. But today he actually seemed glad to go along with it. Like everyone else, he was Peter's now, and Marilyn would be even lonelier now than before Nico came.

She turned around and walked back to find Ward. Maybe he would let her stay with him after all if he knew that the boys had left her. She could see him setting up his easel out near a boat, and then she realized he was not alone. Even from a distance she recognized the lean form of Cassandra sitting there on the wharf beside him. Ward bent down to open his paint box, and Marilyn saw him put one hand under Cassandra's chin as he talked to her.

Marilyn turned around again and went back down the dock the other way. She knew she was feeling sorry for herself, but she had a good reason, and swallowed hard. Peter and Nico would dodge her if she tried to follow them. Ward didn't want her around, and there was nothing to do back home. The air was getting colder, and the loneliness seemed to close in as she walked along the dock, fighting back the tears. Maybe it was time, she thought angrily, to make the family worry about *her* for a change.

Mother was so tied up with Ricky, with coaxing him to do things, that she kept forgetting the others were around. Father always had something to repair or some place to go. And both of them were always worrying about Danny, about whether he was out too far in the water or warm enough or eating too much candy. They were worried about Nico and why he hung around with the surf boys. They didn't seem to worry about Peter, but they were always admiring something he had done— the way he'd trained his pigeon, the windmill he made out in the back yard, the weathervane he put on the roof, the canoe he was making out of a log.

But nobody worried about Marilyn. Sweet old Marilyn, making up the beds and doing the dishes and

128

feeding Ricky and reading to Danny and playing so nicely by herself with her shells and her dumb little sea things —just like Cinderella.

The tears rolled down her cheeks, stinging her face in the wind. She wiped them quickly away with her hand and walked on faster.

"I'll show them," she muttered angrily. "We'll just see! We'll just see!"

She walked over to the water and looked down at the boats. At the bottom of the ladder, a boat was docked. Two men were testing the engine.

"Think she's ready?" one of them called to the other.

"Yeah. She's good for eight hours or more." The man in the plaid shirt straightened up.

"Let's get a bite to eat before we go. Maybe get some sandwiches to carry along," said the other.

They shut off the engine. Then they both climbed up the ladder, past Marilyn, and went to the cafe across the street.

Marilyn knew what she wanted to do, but her legs wouldn't move. She looked around. No one in sight. Suddenly she went to the edge of the dock. With pounding heart, she grasped hold of the ladder, turned around, and lowered herself rung by rung into the boat below.

Her feet made a hollow sound as she stepped down, and the boat tipped a little. The wharf looked so high from where she stood. She could smell the strong odors of tar and oakum, and the briny smell of oysters from a previous catch. With her feet solidly in the boat, she

129

felt brave now and looked around.

She was surrounded by boxes and barrels and lines and pulleys. A trap door in the center of the floor was open, showing more barrels filled with ice. Behind her, on one end of the boat was a small cabin. Marilyn walked over and opened the door.

Inside was an old leather bench, a stove, and a large cupboard from ceiling to floor. The glass windows around the cabin were dirty, and the place smelled of stale coffee and cigars. She opened the bottom of the cupboard, pushed aside the odd assortment of pots and sweaters and raincoats, and climbed in, pulling the door almost shut behind her.

It was warm in the cupboard, almost too warm, and Marilyn had about decided to climb out and find a better place when she felt the boat jerk and heard the voices of the two men.

There was more thumping and bumping around outside. Then the cabin door opened and one of the men came in. He put a sack of sandwiches on the shelf. Marilyn could see his black trousers move about the cabin and then go out. The cabin door slammed, the motor started up, causing a roar in the cabin, and suddenly the boat began to move away from the dock and out to sea.

Each time the boat hit a breaker from another ship, Marilyn bumped her head against the wall. She finally picked up a sweater and put it behind her head to cushion it. As the boat went on, the cupboard began to get warmer and warmer. It felt as though the engine were

directly beneath her, and she could feel every change in vibration as it changed speed, taking Marilyn farther and farther out on the ocean.

She pushed open the cupboard door a little farther to get more air. Now and then she could hear a shout from the men as they moved their gear about and prepared for the long fishing trip ahead.

Now that she was here, Marilyn began to have second thoughts about it. She knew nothing about the two fishermen on board. She would no more have gone in a car with a stranger than jump in a well, and here she had climbed aboard a strange boat with strange people without even thinking. And nobody knew she was here.

Not only that. She was not even sure they were coming back to this town. Maybe they were headed for another state. They had said they would have enough fuel for eight hours, and already the heat from the cupboard was making her dizzy.

She closed her eyes to control her fear. She tried to remember why she got on the boat. Somehow, she had figured that she would wait until she got far out to sea—till her family and the coast guard and police were all looking for her. Then she would tell the crew and they would rush her back, where her weeping parents would be waiting at the dock.

All that was gone now. All Marilyn knew was that she must stay in that cupboard until the boat stopped. Then, when the men were gone, she could sneak out and find her way, somehow, back home.

The heat and the rocking of the boat lulled her into a fitful sleep. Occasionally a shout from one of the men or the clank of boxes would stir her awake momentarily. Then her heart would pound at remembering where she was and she would escape back into sleep again against a background of screeching gulls and the waves lapping the side of the boat.

She was suddenly conscious of the raspy sound of dance music from a transistor radio and she opened her eyes. Her legs ached from the cramped space and there was a pain in her neck. Through a crack in the cupboard door she could see a man's boot and heard the sound of waxed paper crinkling above her.

"What cha want, ham'n'cheese or beef?" said a man's voice.

"Beef," said the other.

There was more rustling of paper and then she could hear the chewing of teeth and smell the aroma of hot coffee.

"Lousy catch," said the first man again.

"Should be better this afternoon south a ways."

"Yeah."

The talk continued—fishing talk.

Marilyn longed for a drink but dared not make a sound. She would wait until the men finished their lunch. Then perhaps she could sneak out and get a drink while they were outside.

The dance music stopped for the weather report. The announcer said it was one-fifteen, then the music began again, loud and raucous.

The boat moved and a piece of crumpled waxed paper fell to the floor. The man got up, and as he did so, bumped his knee on the cupboard door. He swore, and banged the door shut. Then he and the other man went back out.

As soon as they were gone, Marilyn feverishly reached for the lock and tried it. The door wouldn't open. Desperately she ran her hand up and down to find the catch, but it was on the outside of the cupboard. There was no way she could open it from the inside.

Her feverishness gave way to panic. Perspiration rolled down her face and arms as she pushed on the door, banging her head against the top each time she moved. She started to sob, terrified at the thought of suffocating in the hot cupboard, and as the engine started up faster and the air grew hotter, she beat on the door with her fists. Nothing happened. Above the din she could hear the two men calling out to each other but nobody came. Finally, she picked up one of the pans in the corner and beat on the door with all her strength. She beat and beat and beat, sobbing loudly.

Finally, when her arm felt as if it wouldn't move anymore, she heard the cabin door open and a man's voice say, "What the blazes could it be?"

She sobbed again and beat once more upon the door. The cupboard door opened and a strange grizzled face peered inside.

"Holy smoke!"

The two men stood back as Marilyn crawled out, her long red hair matted against her face, her tongue dry, and her eyes swollen.

"Who *is* she?"

"Isn't she the kid who was standing up on the parking lot when we went to lunch?"

"I dunno. I didn't notice."

Marilyn sank down on the leather bench and buried her face in her hands, sobbing loudly.

"Listen, girlie, who are you?" said the man in the red plaid shirt.

"M . . . Marilyn Buckley," Marilyn replied, choking over the words. "I want to g . . . go home. Please!"

There was more silence. Then the man in the gray sweat shirt swore, long and low, under his breath. "We got to take her back, Joe. Only thing to do."

The other man dropped disgustedly down on the folding chair across from Marilyn.

"All the dadburned luck! Halfway out and look what we got." He stared at Marilyn. "How'd you get in the cupboard, kid?"

Marilyn continued to cry and the man asked her again.

"I . . . I crawled in," Marilyn sobbed. "I wanted to run away." She uncovered her face and took the water the other man handed her.

Joe, in the red shirt, glared at her. "I've a mind to finish the trip and make her wait till we get back. It would serve her right. Blasted kid . . .!"

The other man threw up his hands. "We can't do that. They'd slap us with a kidnap charge. We'll probably be in trouble as it is." He looked down at Marilyn. "Your folks at the ocean?"

"Yes."

"They know you're gone?"

"I . . . I suppose they do now."

Joe stood up. "Okay. Let's take her back. Boy, if she was my kid, she wouldn't be able to sit down for a week."

They went out, slamming the door behind them, and pretty soon the boat started to move around in a slow circle and head back.

The men didn't come back in the cabin again. Every time Marilyn looked at them they glared at her, and she was glad they didn't scold her anymore. Everything was bad enough as it was.

It had been over three hours since she had left the house that morning with Ward and Peter and Nico. Peter and Nico should have been home an hour ago, and it would be another two hours before she got back.

Joe came to the door of the cabin only once.

"You cold?" he asked gruffly.

Marilyn shook her head.

"Hungry?"

"No."

"Well, there's a sandwich left if you want it," he said, and shut the door again.

Marilyn felt awful. The men were furious. She had

136

ruined their trip and she wouldn't blame them if they tossed her overboard.

She felt no excitement as the fishing boat entered the harbor and inched its way up to the dock. The motor whined, then stopped, and there was no other sound but the water against the side.

One of the men came over and opened the cabin door. "Okay, kid—out," he said, hardly hiding his disgust.

Marilyn got out. Her face burned. She wanted to thank the men for bringing her back . . . apologize. . . .

"I'm sorry. . . . ," she said hesitantly.

The man waved his hand at her and turned away, too angry to talk.

Marilyn climbed slowly up the ladder, her legs wobbly, careful not to look down at the water below for fear she'd fall in.

There was no one on the parking lot. Marilyn went down the dock to the street, and then down the sidewalk toward the business section. She was so tired she could hardly walk, and she was too exhausted to think. Her feet simply moved. As she got closer to home, more and more things began to look familiar. Finally she was only a block away. She cut over to the beach and started across the long sandy lot that separated the Buckleys from the boardwalk.

She could see Father and Julius standing out in the front yard and Mother up on the porch. Then she heard Peter yell, "There's Marilyn!" from the beach behind

137

her, and a second later he and Nico came running over.

"Where have you been, you goon?" Peter said. *"Everybody's* been looking for you!"

Marilyn didn't answer as Julius and her parents came running across the lot.

"What happened?" said her father, a strange mixture of fury and concern on his face.

But before Marilyn could tell them, her mother asked anxiously, "Where's Danny?"

Danny? Marilyn tried to figure out what they were saying.

"I . . . I don't know."

Mother's face went pale. "Marilyn! Wasn't he with you? Where's Danny?" she repeated.

"I don't know," Marilyn said again. "I . . . I haven't seen him. . . ." Her heart went numb. Danny was gone too. Danny was missing and all afternoon she'd been stowed away on a boat while everyone combed the beach for her and her little brother.

"Oh, Mother!" she cried, terrified.

"It's time to get the police," Father said. "Pat, you come with us this time. Miss Tugberry can stay by the phone. Nico, you and Peter run on down to the coast guard station. I'll call headquarters."

12

Lost

They all headed out in different directions. Marilyn was hardly conscious of her weariness. She was afraid to look at the ocean. Nevertheless, her eyes kept turning toward it, and every time she saw a floating board or a piece of debris, her heart leaped up in her mouth.

She checked every place she could think of—the rocks, the bicycle rental shop, the place Danny sometimes hid beneath the end of the boardwalk. There was no trace of him. Every time she saw a child playing in the sand, she hurried over, but it was never he. There was something special about Danny—the way he said everything that came to mind without polishing it up first; the way he ate peanut butter; the way he sang, "She'll Be Comin' Round the Mountain." All the little things Marilyn had liked before about Danny, she loved now, and her heart ached.

"Have you seen a little four-year-old boy?" she asked various groups of bathers as she passed. "Red hair and freckles?"

Nobody remembered for sure.

"There are so many kids down here," someone said.

One woman thought she might have seen Danny several hours ago, but couldn't remember which way he had been going.

After a while Marilyn saw the others heading back, so she turned and went back too, walking by herself along the water—numb. They met again in the yard, their faces grim.

"The police have two cars out looking for him," Father said. "Let's switch search parties. Those who did the north end of the beach go south this time, and the rest of us will go north."

Mother passed around a pitcher of water which they drank hurriedly.

"It's just not like Danny to go off like this," she said, her voice shaking. "I was so sure he had gone with the rest of you this morning. And then when Peter and Nico came home, I just knew he and Marilyn must have gone somewhere together. I can't imagine. . . . ."

All eyes turned to Marilyn again.

"Where *did* you go, Marilyn?" Father asked. "Peter and Nico said they left you on the dock around eleven-thirty."

Marilyn wished she could cry or sound angry or do anything but just stand there.

"I. . . . hid in a fishing boat . . . and it went out on the ocean before they discovered me," she said, almost inaudibly.

Mr. Buckley stared at her.

"You *what*? Why in the world. . . .? Whose boat?"

"I . . . I don't know. Some men. . . ."

Mrs. Buckley dropped her hands. "Marilyn, have you gone mad?"

At that, the tardy tears welled up in Marilyn's eyes. "Peter and Nico ran off. They didn't want me along," she sobbed, her weariness getting the best of her, her face burning with embarrassment.

Nico looked at Marilyn open-mouthed. "It was to be a surprise," he said.

But Peter was exasperated. "Mar, how dumb can you get? You know what we wanted to do? Buy you a shell bracelet for your birthday next month. We didn't want you to see."

Marilyn's face blanched. She looked from Peter to Nico, her throat dry.

"Marilyn, I . . . I don't understand you, honey!" Mother said, the hurt showing in her eyes. "How could you think . . . ?"

"Look!" Julius pointed down the beach. There came the figures of a man and a woman and a little boy. The woman's steps were long and graceful, and the chubby little legs of the boy could hardly keep up as he clasped her hand and stumbled along beside her.

Mother's hand went to her throat. "Danny!" she cried and, kicking off her shoes, raced across the yard and around the cliff to meet Ward and Cassandra.

They all crowded around, and Cassandra's brown face was full of sympathy.

"You must have been so worried," she said. "I just got home and found Danny asleep in my house. We hurried right over here, and all along the way people told us that he had been missing."

Danny clung sullenly to Cassandra, but as his mother bent down to hug him, he finally let go of Cassandra's hand and buried his head on Mrs. Buckley's shoulder.

Both Mother and Danny were crying. "Danny, darling, where did you go? I thought you were with the other children!"

"They didn't wait for me," Danny sobbed bitterly. "They just went off and lefted me."

"We didn't know you wanted to come," said Peter.

"Marilyn did!" Danny cried accusingly. "She said, 'Hurry before Danny comes.' I heard her."

Marilyn stared at him. Now she remembered. She didn't know Danny had heard. And she didn't think he would try to follow or that he would cry and run away if he were left behind.

142

"Danny, we would have taken you . . . honestly . . . but . . . but . . . you know how you always want to be carried," Marilyn began, hurting because of the hurt she had caused her little brother.

"You never want me to come with you!" Danny bawled. "You always get to do everything! You do! You do! You do!" His voice rose. "You get to feed Ricky and hold him an' you get to make fudge an' you get to plant flowers an' . . an' everything!"

Marilyn could only look at him. She opened her mouth but nothing came out.

"Oh, Danny, what a thing to say!" Mother said, hugging him to her. "Marilyn's our only girl, and of course she gets to do things you and Peter don't, but you *know* how much we love you. . . . ."

"I'll call the police and tell them he's found," said Father. "Why don't you boys run down to the lifeguards and tell them to stop looking."

Mother carried Danny, still sniveling, into the house and Father and Julius went back inside. Ward went down to the shower stall to wash the paint off his arms, leaving Marilyn alone in the front yard with Cassandra.

Marilyn could not bear to look at anyone. She turned away and crawled down the cliff to the beach below, and out on the big rocks along the shore. The afternoon sun was low in the sky, and there were few people on the beach—only the sandpipers that scurried out on the sand and back again as the breakers came in, never getting their little feet wet. She hated herself and

144

she felt that everybody else hated her, too.

Someone sat down on the rocks beside her. Marilyn saw the long brown legs of Cassandra stretched out to the water, her leather sandals dangling in her hand.

"Sort of a bad day, isn't it?" said the tall woman, her voice gentle.

"It's awful," said Marilyn. "I . . . I just hate myself."

Cassandra nodded. "That's a bad feeling. When one hates himself he hates the world. It even makes the ocean look black."

It was true. The ocean never looked darker.

"Someone said that you too were missing all day," said Cassandra. "What happened after you left Ward on the dock?"

"I thought Peter and Nico didn't want me along, so I got on a fishing boat that was just going out. And all the time Peter and Nico wanted to buy me a present. Now everybody's angry—the fishermen were angry at me, my family, Danny . . . And the worst is that Danny ran away because he heard *me* say I didn't want *him* along."

The tears were rolling down Marilyn's cheeks again, and suddenly she leaned her head against Cassandra's blue jacket and cried hard. The brown beachcomber put her arm around Marilyn and waited until the tears were over.

"Haven't you enjoyed your summer here, Marilyn?" she asked.

"I . . . I guess so . . . yes and no," Marilyn said. "But I was afraid of it—coming here. I was afraid to have Nico in the family. I mean, now there are four boys." She sat up straight. "I don't think Nico wants to be my special friend. Or Peter's either. I don't know what he wants to be."

"Of course he doesn't," said Cassandra. "Not even a girl wants to be that special. No one can ever own anybody else completely, for that would not be love at all. No matter how much you like a friend, you must always leave him a little bit free to be whatever he likes."

Cassandra smiled down at her. "It is like the ocean and me. I have lived here all my life, so long that I sometimes feel that it belongs to me. I know its tides and its breakers and every rock along the shore. I know when the water will be warmest. I know its winds and its currents and the stars that shine over it at night. I know it so well that just when I am sure I know it completely, it surprises me. It shows that it is master of itself, and beats against my house until it knocks it down. Then I understand that however much we like each other, the ocean and I, I cannot own it and it cannot own me either."

It sounded so strange, hearing the sunburned gypsy talk about the ocean as though it were a person. It sounded so much like Nico. Maybe he too wanted to show them all that he was master of himself.

Mrs. Buckley and Ward came across the sand.

"I don't know where my manners are," Mother said

146

to Cassandra. "I was so upset about the children being gone that I didn't even thank you for bringing Danny back."

"I can understand," Cassandra said, giving Ward a warm smile. "I don't know how long he was in my house, because I was gone for several hours. But I always leave the door unlocked during the day, and there were raisins and marshmallows in the cupboard. He must have had a wonderful time before he fell asleep."

"We'll be eating soon," Mother said. "Can't you stay and have dinner with us? The children—we all— would love to have you."

"We had other plans for the evening, Mrs. Buckley," Ward said, smiling. "But ask her again. I'll see to it that she comes."

"I certainly will," said Mother. "And soon."

Ward turned to Cassandra. "I think I'm presentable. All the paint came off except the green blob on my ear, and that's in six layers."

They said good-bye and went off down the beach. Mrs. Buckley sat down beside Marilyn and watched them go. They quietly listened to the gulls and the breakers, and watched Ward and Cassandra grow smaller and smaller. Maybe, thought Marilyn, happy with Mother there beside her, you have to be patient about the time and the love other people give you. Maybe, if you just wait and not beg for it, people will give you what they can of themselves.

Mother put one arm around Marilyn and hugged

her tight. "Marilyn, we love you," she said. "*Please* don't . . ."

"I won't, Mother," Marilyn said emphatically. "I promise I'll never run away again—ever."

Far down the beach, Marilyn saw Ward slip one arm around Cassandra, and the barefoot gypsy moved closer to him as they walked.

"Mother, do you think they are in love?" Marilyn asked.

Mrs. Buckley smiled. "It is hard to tell about these things. We'll have to wait and see."

13

Fly Away Home

The day was hot and sultry. The wind was so weak it
could scarcely blow the stray cups that were strewn along
the beach. The usual sun-lovers were lying on the sand,
baking their bodies to an even all-over brown. But most
of the beachcombers preferred to stay inside and wait
until the evening breeze blew in.

There was a scuffling on the back porch of Cliff
House. Danny came screeching through the kitchen,
grabbed at Marilyn's skirt for protection, and raced on
through the living room and out the front door with Peter
on his heels.

"Peter!" Mother yelled from the stairs. "What on earth. . . . ?"

"Mommy! He's going to hit me!" Danny yelped as Peter tackled him in the front yard. "Ma-ma!"

Mr. Buckley came around the side of the house. "Peter! Get off! What's going on?"

Peter tumbled off and sat glaring at his younger brother. "He was in my pigeon cage again and he didn't even shut the door."

"Listen, Danny, we've told you before to leave the pigeon alone," said Father. "If you do it again and anything happens to Peter's bird, you'll have to save your money to buy him another. Do you understand?"

"I wasn't going to hurt her!" Danny insisted. "I was just feedin' her a worm and she liked it, too."

Nico came home a few minutes later with his surf board and clanked it against the side of the house as he kicked off his beach sandals.

"I'm through with those guys," he said, and Marilyn stared down at him from the porch.

Mr. Buckley dipped his brush in the paint bucket again and went on painting the trim on the basement windows. "The surf boys?"

"Yes."

"Why? What happened?"

"Everything they do I must do or they are angry," said Nico. "So now *I* am angry. I do not like to be the dog that comes when someone whistles."

"I don't blame you," said Father, and Marilyn could

150

tell how glad he was to hear Nico say that.

It was just that sort of day. Tongues were dry, tempers were short, and everybody had a gripe. It was even too hot to go in the ocean. When the young Buckleys tried it, the glare of the sun on the glittering water burned their shoulders each time as they stood up. After a while they gave that up too and came dripping and scowling to the front porch where they plopped down lifelessly on the straw mats, waiting for the afternoon breeze.

The breeze from the ocean came at last, and soon became a wind. As evening wore on, the wind became a gale. By eight o'clock, the rain came down in torrents.

"Is it another hurricane?" Danny asked as he stood at the screen.

"Nope. It's a northeaster, and it's going to be a honey!" said Father.

"Poseidon is angry and makes the oceans roar," said Nico.

"Who?" asked Marilyn.

"The god of the sea," Nico explained, smiling. "It is an old Greek myth."

On the beach the gale warnings were up. All the artists had gone back to Pennsylvania now except Ward, and the near-empty rooms shook and rattled their doors. Nico and Peter hid in the closets and yelled, "Ah-oooh!" when Danny came by, and it was all Mother could do to get Danny to bed that night.

The next morning the sky was gray and the air was cold with a touch of autumn. One more week before

151

school began, and they would be leaving soon for the big yellow house back in Wheaton. Nico would either go with them or fly back to Greece. No one knew for sure.

The family was just finishing breakfast. Peter had gone out to feed his pigeon and Danny was drawing a truck on his plate with strawberry jam. Suddenly there was a yell from the back yard, a thud of feet, and Peter appeared in the doorway, his eyes wild and his fists clenched.

"Who did it?" he yelled, bolting inside. "Who let my pigeon out? She's dead!"

The others gasped.

"Oh, no!" said Mother. "Danny, did you. . . .?"

"I didn't touch that old bird!" Danny declared.

"Who fed her last?" Peter demanded, crazy with anger.

Nico looked up slowly. "I did, Peter. I guess I forgot to lock the door to the cage and the wind blew it open. I'm sorry. . . . ."

Peter whirled around. "You creep! You lousy creep!"

"Peter!" said Mother.

Peter could hardly keep back the tears. "Good gosh, Mother, a gale blowing and Nico leaves the door unlocked! Of all the dumb jerks . . ."

"Peter, I'm sorry. . . ," Nico began again.

"That doesn't get my bird back, does it?" Peter snapped. "If she'd been in the cage she could have gone in the shelter I built for her. Instead she was trying to

152

fly and the wind smashed her against our house."

"Nico will have to buy you another one," said Mr. Buckley.

"I . . . I don't have a dollar," said Nico. "Only sixty cents."

"I'll lend you the rest so you can buy Peter's bird before we leave," Father told him. "You'll have to do without ice cream money for the rest of the week, I guess."

Nico did not answer. But Marilyn, watching from across the table, was shocked. How could Father do that to Nico? He hadn't meant to let Peter's bird out. Nobody liked ice cream better than Nico did. He'd never want to live with them now!

They buried the bird in the sand beside the porch, and Danny tearfully placed a popsickle stick over the grave.

Nico was gone two hours before he found the man who sold birds, and he brought one back and gave it to Peter without a word.

"Thanks," Peter said gruffly, then added, "I was really mad at you this morning."

"I know," said Nico.

Bundled up in a sweater, Marilyn walked along the shore. The more she thought about Nico, the more she knew she would miss him. They could have had so much fun back in Wheaton—riding bicycles around the neighborhood, going out on Halloween, decorating the Christmas tree . . . If Nico decided to go back to Greece, maybe Mother and Father would never get a sister for Marilyn.

Her eyes, like faucets, filled, and she began to bawl. "What's the matter?"

A sob caught in her throat, and Marilyn tried quickly to swallow it as she looked up on the cliff. There, of all people, was Nico.

"Your eyes are as red as your sweater," he said.

The way he said it almost made her laugh. But her chin bobbed up and down instead and suddenly Marilyn's mouth opened wide and she wailed, "I don't want you to go back to Greece."

Nico looked at her strangely. "Someone is sending me back?"

"Of course n . . . not. But you're going, aren't you?"

Nico smiled and slid down the cliff. He picked up a few rocks and skipped them out over the water. "No," he said simply. "I want to stay. I have decided. I am going to be Nicolos Panagiolis Buckley. How does that sound?"

Marilyn stared at the dark-haired boy. She couldn't believe it! Then, with a shriek, she ran around the cliff to the house, waving her arms and yelling all the way to tell the good news.

Nicolos Panagiolis Buckley just smiled and skipped another stone on the ocean.

Cassandra came to dinner on Saturday night.

"Our best dishes, Mother!" Marilyn commented, looking at the pretty table with a big bowl of yellow flowers in the center of it and candles on either side. "Is

155

this something special?"

Mother smiled. "It could be. Now I'd like you to make place cards for each plate. And put Ward and Cassandra side by side."

As the sun was sinking behind the town and the sky over the ocean turned dark, Cassandra arrived at Cliff House. She had on a pretty cotton dress with a big coral necklace and coral earrings in her ears. Her long black hair had been wrapped high on top of her head. Marilyn could hardly believe it was the same lady.

Danny, too, was surprised. "Why, Cassandra, you're almost *purty!*" he declared.

And Ward answered, "Wrong, Danny boy. She's beautiful."

Mother was right, Marilyn thought, noting the way Ward looked at Cassandra. This was a special night.

It was like a big Thanksgiving dinner. Julius and Miss Tugberry and Ward and Cassandra seemed like members of the family.

"That is a beautiful necklace, Cassandra," Julius said. "I knew a young girl who was fond of coral. I gave her a coral pin once, and do you know where she wore it? In her hair. It was lovely!"

Cassandra smiled, and Miss Tugberry said, "Was that the girl you told us about, Julius? Did you ever tell the others about all the excitement we had here one day?"

Marilyn and Peter and Nico looked at each other. They had been trying to keep Julius' secret, and now Miss Tugberry gave it away.

156

Julius looked around. "Well, I guess it's not a secret any longer. And since I'm among friends, I can't see any harm in telling."

"Good heavens," said Mother, "What happened?"

So Julius told the story again of his young sweetheart, Alice, and how he had recently found a message in the bottle by the stump.

"How odd!" said Mother. "After thirty-three years, who could possibly recognize you except Alice?"

"We'll never know the answer," said Julius. "The stump is buried, and I'll be leaving in a few days. I never thought, when I came back for a vacation, that it would start the whole thing all over again."

Later, as Mother cut the peach shortcake, Ward said, "Mrs. Buckley, would you care if I used this moment to make an announcement?"

And before Mother could open her mouth, Marilyn and Peter and Nico cried, "Ward and Cassandra are getting married!"

"How about that?" said Ward, as Cassandra threw back her dark head and laughed. "Can't keep a single secret in this house!"

"When is the big day?" said Mother. "And where?"

"You'll never guess," said Ward. "Tomorrow. Here —if you'll let us."

"Here? Tomorrow!" cried everybody.

"Of course you may," said Mother. "Oh, won't this be exciting!"

There was so much to do that dinner ended early.

Everybody wanted a part in the wedding. Julius agreed to give the bride away, Miss Tugberry promised to sing, and the children were rushing up and down the stairs getting things ready. Ward and Cassandra left early as a big orange moon rose over the water.

Marilyn had gone upstairs to get some extra vases and was just passing Julius' room when she saw a piece of paper taped to his door.

"Julius," it said. "Go to the pier to the fourth pillar down, turn right and count 52 paces, turn right again and count 20, cross the inlet and at the third large rock, turn left. There you will find your answers."

"Peter!" Marilyn whispered from the stairway. "Come quick!"

Peter came upstairs. "What is it?"

"Look! The note on Julius' door. The mystery person has been here while we all had dinner!"

Peter's eyes grew wide. "I'll bet Julius will go tonight, as soon as he finds this. C'mon. Let's get Nico and we'll follow him."

They didn't think Julius would ever go upstairs that night. He sat around watching television. Then he went out on the porch and smoked his pipe, went down the steps and looked up at the stars, came back in and read the sports section of the newspaper.

"Okay, kids," Father said at ten o'clock. "To bed. It's a big day tomorrow, and Mother will want you to help with the house."

Marilyn started to protest, but Peter said, "C'mon."

158

At the top of the stairs he told her, "Let's stay dressed. As soon as Julius comes up, we'll all slip out the side door and follow him."

It wasn't long before Julius came upstairs. Marilyn heard his footsteps echoing down the hall to his room. And then they stopped abruptly. There was a long pause, so long Marilyn wondered if he was still there. Then he hurried on into his room, put on his raincoat, and moved softly down the front stairs and out the front door.

"Now!" Marilyn whispered to Nico and Peter, rushing back up to the third floor. They pulled on their sweaters and stole down the side steps.

Julius went straight down the boardwalk. So as not to be seen, Marilyn and Nico and Peter went out across the sand and walked along by the ocean in the darkness. Once or twice they thought they had lost him, but then they saw him moving on ahead.

Twenty minutes later they reached the pier, and crouched down behind the rocks along the shore. Julius left the boardwalk and walked down between the rows of pillars beneath the pier. One . . . two . . . three . . . four. . . . The fourth pillar. He turned right and began pacing steadily off through the sand. One, two, three, four, five, six. . . . . He had fifty-two steps to go and the children scrambled up to the weeds on the bank and crawled along above him.

Finally Julius stopped and read the directions again. Then he turned right and the children flattened themselves down on the sand so he wouldn't see them as he passed by. This time he counted twenty paces. He came to a small inlet, several feet across, which he jumped. Then he passed by three large rocks and stopped again.

"Is that all?" Peter asked. "Is he there?"

"Cassandra's house!" Nico whispered.

Julius was confused. He looked around. Suddenly the door opened wide and the glow of a lamp shone out on the sand.

"Come in, Julius," said Cassandra, smiling. "I've been expecting you."

"Expecting me?" asked Julius. As he entered the house, Marilyn could see Ward inside. The door closed again.

Marilyn scrambled to her feet. "Maybe we can peek in the window."

They ran through the scrubby grass to the little stream and jumped across. Then, crawling over the big rocks, they crouched under the window and tried to peep through the hopsack curtains.

"Quit shoving, Peter," said Nico.

"Who's shoving? I'm trying to see up over the top."

"Be quiet," Marilyn scolded. "Somebody will. . . ."

The door opened and Ward came out.

"Well, well, well, the three detectives," he said.

Julius came to the door and peered over his shoulder.

"I *knew* they'd come," said Cassandra, laughing. "That's why I taped the note to the door instead of sticking it underneath!"

But as the children edged sheepishly into the one-

160

room house, Julius looked as surprised as they were. "What goes on?" he asked.

"Ah, Julius, I could not leave here without telling you," said Cassandra. "I decided to have a little fun out of it. Sit down at the table, all of you. I have just enough tea for one cup each, and some rather good biscuits. Then I will tell you all you want to know."

She took the kettle off the hot plate in one corner and poured the steaming tea into six cracked cups.

"*You* put the note on my door?" said Julius. "Then it was you who put the messages in the bottle?"

"Yes, it was I."

Julius stared at her. "But how did you know about the stump and the messages I used to send Alice?"

Cassandra sat down and looked at Julius through the steam that rose from her cup. "Alice was my mother."

Julius stared at her, his mouth open. "Alice—your mother?" he asked. "Is she . . . . still alive?"

"No, Julius. She died many years ago."

Julius looked soberly down into his cup. Nobody spoke. Marilyn was almost afraid to swallow for fear even that would make too much noise.

"Tell me the rest," Julius said finally.

"My father was a sea captain. My grandparents did not want Mother to marry you because . . . because they thought you might not be able to provide all the things she had been used to having."

Julius smiled. "That's true," he murmured. "But I did love her."

161

"And she you," Cassandra added. "When her parents found out that you and she wanted to marry, they sent her to a girls' school in North Carolina for three years. When she finally came back, she met a young man who worked for a shipping company, and they were married. As a wedding present, my grandparents gave them the house where my mother lived as a girl—the house the Buckleys own now. And there it was that I was born and raised, just as my mother had been." She looked at Marilyn. "In fact, my room was exactly the one that you have now."

Cassandra's face grew serious again and she stopped to sip her tea. "The rest of the story, I'm afraid, is not so happy. My father used to be gone on long voyages— sometimes two months. My mother knew of his love for the sea before they were married, but perhaps she felt she could change him. The days were lonely. Mother and I used to sit on the porch and watch the breakers come in. She would tell me about the things she had done as a girl. That was how I learned about you, Julius.

"She showed me your picture and told me of the wonderful summer you had together. She even told me about the notes in the bottle by the stump, and when I was small, I used to hide notes there, too, always wondering if you might come back and dig them up.

"My father was as big and strong as Mother was small and weak. He loved the wind and the stars and, when he was home, he and I spent long hours walking along the shore, picking up shells, and exploring the

162

dock. Finally, when I was sixteen, my mother felt she could stand the ocean no longer. After a great deal of tears and pleading, she persuaded my father to give up the work he loved so much.

"We moved to Baltimore, but my father was unhappy. He wanted to come back and spend our summers here, but Mother didn't. So they turned our house at the ocean into a boarding house and sold it. A year later, my father died, and a year after that, my mother. They both loved each other, and yet . . . they each made the other unhappy."

Cassandra reached up and unwound her hair, letting it fall loose and long down her back. "I am like my father, I guess. When I was twenty, I left college and came here. I bought this little house—a fisherman's shack all painted blue and white—and became the gypsy."

The wind howled outside around the chipped blue shutters and even the walls seemed to shake. But all was quiet in the little house.

"How did you know I was in town?" Julius asked.

"I saw you get off the bus. I was shopping at the market, and I was afraid you would wonder at me, I stared so. Even though you are older, you looked so much like the pictures Mother had of you. I followed you, and when I saw you go directly to the Buckley's house, I was certain. I wondered if you would look for a message after all these years, so I wrote one and hid it by the stump. A week later, I was walking along the beach at midnight and I dug up the bottle again. I was so surprised when I

163

found you had answered my note. A little later I left you another. Then came the hurricane, and the stump was buried."

Julius sat for a long time looking down at his empty tea cup. "Life is strange," he said at last. "After thinking about Alice all these years, and never marrying anyone else . . . is it possible that I too might have been unhappy with her? And she with me?"

"Yes, it is possible," said Cassandra. "It is not good to go one's whole life just living a dream. My grandparents were wealthy, and they gave my mother many things. I am not sure she would have been happy being the wife of a shoe salesman in Buffalo and giving music lessons. But not all women are alike. Some would be delighted to do it, you know."

"Well," said Julius finally, smiling at the couple beside him. "So now Ward is taking you away from the ocean to live in Philadelphia?"

"We made a compromise," said Ward. "I would not be happy spending my whole life here away from the city. And Cassandra would not be happy forever in Philadelphia." He turned to the children. "You detectives—be our witnesses! I, Ward Evans, do solemnly swear that I shall return to the ocean with my bride every summer, from here to eternity, to fulfill her gypsy soul."

Julius shook their hands. "My best wishes to you both," he said. "Cassandra, you have satisfied a long curiosity. And now I shall leave."

"I'm coming, too," said Ward. "Cassandra has a lot

164

to do to get ready for the wedding."

Julius and the children set back out across the beach, and Ward caught up with them shortly.

"If your parents missed you, they'll have the whole coast guard out this time," Ward said, pulling Nico's ear. "I don't know how three kids can get into as much trouble as you do."

"They could be worse," said Julius. "Look up there."

A row was going on up on the boardwalk. The surf boys were up to something. Several bleached heads disappeared in all directions as two policemen ran around the corner of the building.

It's a good thing Nico wasn't with them, Marilyn thought, as the boardwalk grew quiet once more.

"Thought you used to be buddies with those fellas, Nico," Ward said.

"Not really friends," said Nico, and Marilyn waited, wondering. "Sometimes, when one is treated very specially—I do not know how to say it—it is good to get away where one is not special at all—just to see—if one can get along. Do you not know?"

Ward nodded in the darkness. "Yes, I think I can understand that. It is no challenge to be only with those who think that everything we do is wonderful, nice as that is. That's why I sometimes enter my pictures in galleries where I know they will be ripped apart by the critics—just to see if I can take it. But if things get too tough, I can always send my pictures home to Mom." He laughed. "She thinks they're great."

165

They arrived home just as Mr. Buckley was locking the front screen for the night. He stared aghast, thinking they were all in bed. "Where have you been?" he thundered.

"Peace!" said Julius, holding up his hand. "Let the children go to bed, sir, and I shall tell you a most fascinating story."

Marilyn would have liked to stay up and hear it all over again, but she was too tired. So she gave in without a whimper, and the next thing she knew she was dreaming that Cassandra was coming into the room in a long white gown, riding on the back of Miss Tugberry's goat.

14

Wedding March

The sun rose high over the water bright and warm, as though the ocean were just made for weddings. Ward left the house early to get bus tickets and a haircut and to pick up the coral ring he had ordered for Cassandra.

All day long the children gathered wild flowers from the sandy lots on down the beach, till the living room of Cliff House looked like a flower store. Miss Tugberry sat at the old piano and sang, "Oh, Promise Me," till Mr. Buckley moaned under his breath that he could not stand it one more time, and the children giggled.

167

At six o'clock, every bathtub in the big house had somebody in it. Mother sent Nico and Peter and Danny down to take a shower in the outdoor stall under the house. Marilyn gave Ricky a bath in the kitchen sink.

"Look, Mother, how he holds onto the washcloth," Marilyn said. "He never did that before."

Mother came over and looked. She smiled at Ricky and poked her finger in his fat little belly. "I believe he likes the water," she said. "Tomorrow we'll take him down on the beach and set him where the waves can roll up on his legs. The water is quite warm now."

That was funny about the ocean. By the time the water was warm enough to swim in without making teeth chatter, school was starting and it was time to go back home.

Marilyn gently ran the washcloth over Ricky's head. He would need so much love. It was easy to love him now, when he was small and cute. But how would she feel about him when he was as old as Peter? Could she love him even then, when people stared and whispered and laughed behind his back? Then he would need it even more.

"Oh, Ricky," she promised, picking his wet little body up and hugging it close to her. "I'll always love you—just because you're you and for no other reason. Just because you're you."

By seven o'clock, everything was ready. The Buckleys had on their best clothes. The living room and front porch were filled with pink-hatted ladies and black-

168

suited men who had come to wish the new couple well.

The minister arrived in his black robe, and a few minutes later Mother sat down at the piano and played "Oh, Promise Me," for the last time. Miss Tugberry tipped her head way back as she sang and closed her eyes and her lips trembled up and down with her wavery voice. She had on a bright purple dress with tassels at the sleeves, and somehow Marilyn pictured her as a seal balancing a ball on her nose at the circus. But she dared not laugh, and at last the song was over. Then Mother began to play, "Here Comes the Bride." Cassandra came in the side door on Julius' arm, her face brown against her white summer dress, and her eyes as twinkly as the stars over the ocean.

For the first time, Marilyn could see that Cassandra was truly beautiful, not the way the girls in magazines are beautiful, but beautiful because there was no other woman in the whole world quite like her.

Cassandra walked to the bottom of the stairs where Ward was waiting. She put out her hand, Ward took it, and they stood in front of the minister while he pronounced them man and wife.

As soon as the ceremony was over, everyone began crowding around them. Ward put his arm around his new wife and kissed her hard and got lipstick all over his mouth, while Danny giggled loudly.

Mother winked at Marilyn. "Now!" she whispered. Marilyn crept up the stairs to the landing, picked up a big basket, and emptied it over the railing. Down fluttered

170

a thousand flowers over hats and veils and shiny bald heads.

"Cassandra," said Mother, "there wasn't time to get a wedding gift for you and Ward. Could you think of something you would really like that we could mail to you?"

"Oh, Mrs. Buckley, do you know what I want most of all? That captain's bell in the corner was my father's, from his ship. Mother thought it was ugly and wanted it left here when we sold this house. I would so love to have it now."

"Of course you may," said Mother. "You're the very one who should have it. Ward gave us the key to your little house so we could check it just before we go. I'll have the children take the bell over there tomorrow."

"Where are you going on your honeymoon?" everyone wanted to know, but of course Ward wouldn't tell. "That's one secret you'll never find out," he said, shaking his fist at Peter and Nico.

"You know," Cassandra said to Marilyn, "it's been years since I was in this house. Would you mind very much if I took a look around my old room before I go?"

"Oh, please come up," said Marilyn, happy to have the bride all to herself for a moment.

They slipped away from the crowd and went up the two flights of stairs to the third floor.

"Just think," Cassandra said as they went down the hall to the back bedroom, "Mother had this room when she was small, then I had it, and now it's yours. I always liked it because of the laundry chute."

"What laundry chute?" Marilyn asked as they went in.

Cassandra looked around. "Why . . . they've closed it up." She walked over to the wall and ran her hand over it. "It used to be right here. There was a little door that opened up, and I could drop my clothes down it for the maid to wash."

Marilyn's eyes were wide. "Oh, Cassandra! There's somebody in that old chute!"

"Somebody *in* it!" said Cassandra.

At that moment, as if on cue, there was a *tap* . . . *tap tap tap* . . . *tap* . . . *tap* . . . from the wall.

"There!" cried Marilyn excitedly. "That is what I've been hearing. Somebody is knocking."

"Why, it's the captain!" said Cassandra.

"A captain—in my wall?"

Cassandra laughed a little, but her face was puzzled. "My father and I had a game. It was a long way up to third floor from first, and when he wanted me to come to dinner, he often stood at the bottom of the stairs and yelled. We decided we needed a quiet signal. So I tied a shell onto the end of a rope and hooked it to a nail in the clothes chute. The other end of the rope went all the way down beneath the house where our maid did the washing. Then, no matter where my father was, on second floor or first, all he had to do when he wanted me was to open the clothes chute on each floor and jiggle the rope.

172

When I heard it, I would say, 'There's the captain calling.' Oh, we had a whole set of signals worked out. Two taps meant dinner time. Three meant he was ready for our evening walk. Four meant that. . . ."

Tap . . . tap tap . . . tap tap tap. . . .

Marilyn and Cassandra looked at each other. "But who's signaling now?" Cassandra said. "Who could possibly know about this old chute in the wall . . . ?" And suddenly she said, "Let's go see."

They hurried down to second floor. The chute led through Ward's room, but it had been plastered over, just as it was in Marilyn's room. They went to the kitchen. There, too, it had been sealed up.

"Now what are you up to?" asked Ward, following them out on the back porch.

"Somebody's hiding in the house!" said Marilyn excitedly.

"And sending messages," said Cassandra.

Ward rolled his eyes. "Not again! Not on our wedding day!"

"But we heard it, both of us," said Cassandra. "Come on, darling. Let's look under the house."

So Ward went down the back steps with them and around to the side.

Cassandra peered into the darkness beneath the house. "The chute came out somewhere back under there. The maid kept her wash tubs there, and the clothes would drop right in." Suddenly she grabbed Ward's arm. "Someone's under there!" she whispered.

173

"What's going on?" said Mr. Buckley, looking down from the porch with Peter and Nico.

"Somebody's under your house, Mr. Buckley, and the girls say he's sending messages," said Ward. "Got a flashlight?"

"What's this? What's this?" asked Julius, hurrying out of the kitchen with Mrs. Buckley.

"I'll know in a minute," said Ward. He took the flashlight Father handed him and, ducking his head, stepped under the porch and snapped the light on.

Maaaaaa, said the prowler beneath the house. *Maaaaaaa.*

"Sylvia!" cried Marilyn.

Ward laughed loudly. "It's Sylvia, all right—chewing on a rope and minding her own business. Now will you ladies please tell us what kind of messages this goat has been sending?"

Marilyn and Cassandra leaned on each other in laughter.

"Of course!" said Cassandra. "When Sylvia chewed on that rope, it rattled the shell in Marilyn's wall."

"*What* shell? *What* wall?" Nico wanted to know, and Marilyn had to tell the whole story.

Mother sat down on the back steps. "Ralph," she said laughing, "I don't think I could take another summer like this. If we have one more mystery around here. . . ."

"Why, we're only getting started!" said Father. "Think of all the summers ahead!"

174

"There's one mystery left," said Peter. "The first night we were here, Marilyn and Danny and I saw something, or someone, in our front yard. It looked like a statue. Then it disappeared."

"That is no mystery," said Cassandra. "That was me. I had heard that a family had bought the house. I was so happy to think that children would be here, living in the rooms I had lived in, that I couldn't resist coming by and peeping in. Then I saw you children up in the window and I was afraid you would see me. So I hurried off."

"We thought you were a ghost," said Marilyn. "We thought the house was haunted."

"Oh, but it is," Cassandra told her. "It is haunted with memories. This is the most wonderful house on the coast."

Maaaaaa, went Sylvia again, coming out from under the porch and nuzzling Cassandra. *Maaaaaa.*

Cassandra took a flower from the cluster in her hair and fed it to Sylvia. "Here, beautiful white one," she said. "May your hair grow long and sleek and your belly fat. I hope you have enjoyed your stay at the ocean as much as I have enjoyed this summer."

Finally it was time for the newlyweds to leave. Everyone drove to the bus station to see them off.

"It's been so nice having you with us this summer, Ward," Mrs. Buckley smiled warmly. "Our very best wishes for you and your bride."

"Till next summer, then," said Ward. "Cassandra

and I will be living in her little house on the beach—paints, easel, and all. Now to find an apartment in Philadelphia for the rest of the year."

"What about you, Julius?" asked Father. "Will you be with us again next summer?"

Julius smiled and shook his head. "No, not again. It was a good vacation, but now my search is over. Now I live for the future, not the past, and I must begin with the friendships I have, not a dream."

"And what about you, Miss Tugberry?"

"That is a good question," said the little old lady. "I haven't the slightest idea what Sylvia and I will be doing then. We may be off to Hawaii for all I know. But some day we will be back."

Marilyn walked over to the door of the bus beside Cassandra, and the new bride put her arm around the red-haired girl.

"Enjoy the best your friends have to offer, Marilyn, and do not ask for their souls, too," said Cassandra. "Their hearts are enough." She bent down and kissed her, and Marilyn's lips trembled as Ward and Cassandra boarded the bus. Without knowing it, she and Cassandra had become the very best of friends.

"Wasn't it a beautiful wedding?" Mrs. Buckley sighed as the family drove back to Cliff House. "I can hardly wait to see them again next year. But I'll miss Julius and Miss Tugberry, won't you, Ralph?"

Father nodded. "But we'll have other boarders. The art colony is coming back again, and who knows who

176

else? That's what keeps it interesting. We never know· what excitement they'll bring."

Marilyn sat quietly in a corner of the back seat, thinking over what Cassandra had said. Whenever the black-haired woman talked, it sounded like a poem, and she did not always understand it. But she felt she understood this time. Maybe now that Danny and Ricky and Nico were in the family, she would have to learn to love all over again, loving a person for what he was instead of thinking how much he could give you. Maybe the best place to start was with Ricky, who couldn't give anything at all, who needed to be loved just because he was alive.

"I don't understand it, Daddy," said Marilyn, three days before they went home. "All summer long we were extra nice to Nico, and he didn't know if he wanted to be adopted or not. Then you made him pay for Peter's bird, and he decided to stay."

Father smiled as he took down the porch swing and put the screws in his pocket. "Maybe that's what he wanted all along—to feel like a part of the family. As long as we treated him special, he probably felt that he had to *be* special, and nobody likes to feel that way all the time."

The Buckleys had promised to take the old captain's bell to Cassandra's cabin. Father loaded it in Danny's wagon.

"Make sure the doors and windows are locked tightly," he said, giving Nico the key.

Peter and Marilyn went too. It was a cool crisp afternoon. The wind was full of sand, and the few people on the beach had towels wrapped around their heads to keep the sand out of their hair. The gulls circling around overhead seemed to know that the season was over and soon they would have the beach to themselves.

The wind whistled around their ears as they neared the pier, and they drank deeply of the salt-wood smell, knowing they would not enjoy it again until next summer. The tall scrubby grass on the bank beyond swayed in the wind, and a gull flew squawking out of the weeds.

They climbed the bank and walked along in the brush until they came to the narrow inlet, where the ocean sat cool and clear. They leaped across, pulling the wagon through the shallow water, and made their way through the huge rocks on the other side.

Suddenly Peter stopped. "Listen."

There were noises inside Cassandra's cabin—a bang and a thud and the low murmur of boys' voices.

"Somebody's in there!" said Marilyn.

"Come on," said Nico. He walked over to the cabin and threw open the front door, which had been pried open from the outside.

Four boys were there. They jerked around when they heard the door open, and one of them sneered, "Well! Look who's here! Greaseball and his friends."

The way the boy said it—his lips turned down at the corners—his teeth showing, made Marilyn's legs tremble. What was Nico going to do against four older boys?

178

One of them moved closer. "Thought you were through with us, grease. What'cha come back for, a punch in the nose?"

"We came to see that the cabin was locked," said Nico. "We have the key." He went on in, pulling the wagon behind him. After he and Peter had lifted the huge bell onto the table, Nico walked back to the door, held it open, and said, "Please get out."

The big boy laughed loudly. "*Please* get out," he mimicked. "Hey, guys, the Greek said 'please.' "

"It's not your house either," said another boy. "You can't fool us. You came here to see what you could get your dirty fingers on. All Greeks have sticky fingers."

"Cassandra asked us to check her cabin," Peter said. "You guys better leave."

Marilyn quaked. Peter, too? What did they think they could do—take on an army? She could see past the door. Already the surf boys had pulled down the curtains and thrown things out of the cupboards.

"Peter!" she said softly. "Let's go get somebody."

"Listen, sister, you're not going to get anybody," said a big boy, stepping out the door. Marilyn turned and ran back up the bank. The boy ran after her, grabbing her arm so hard she fell down. Marilyn screamed.

"Hey!" the boy shouted to the others. "Carrot-top here was gonna squeak. Maybe she needs a haircut, too."

"Like we gave the goat," laughed another boy, coming out. "Yeah! Let's make it good and short."

In an instant, Peter hurled himself across the sand,

179

landing on the boy's back, and Nico lunged for the boy standing over Marilyn. A second later they were both grappling on the ground. Marilyn shrieked again, and the other two surf boys ran out, grabbed her, and pushed her inside the cabin, holding the door shut from the outside.

Marilyn began to sob. Nico and Peter would be beaten badly, and no one could see down here where the cabin nestled between the rocks and the beach. Nor would anyone hear if she screamed.

Suddenly her eye fell on the old captain's bell on the table. She looked around and her heart pounded. Quickly she tiptoed over to the front door and bolted the door from the inside. She opened a back window wide, checking to make sure the screen was locked. Then, shaking so badly she could scarcely move, she picked up the old rope on the bell and pulled with all her might.

Clang, clang, clang.

"Hey!" yelled the boys outside, and tried to open the door. It wouldn't budge. They beat on the door, yelled some more, and went running around the house to see if they could get in a window.

Clang, clang, clang. The bell shook the four walls of the cabin.

One of the boys outside swore. "Stop it!" he yelled.

But Marilyn kept on. *Clang, clang, clang, clang, clang, clang. . . .* She pulled with all her might, and the huge bell swung violently back and forth in its stand.

"C'mon," she heard one of the boys shout. "She'll

180

have the whole coast guard down here."

She heard the sound of running feet, and then a man's voice yell, "Hold it! Stay right there." She looked out and saw two policemen coming down the bank, sticks in hand. She ran to the door and unlocked it.

Nico was standing by the house, rubbing the back of his neck. Peter was sitting on the ground. There was blood on his shirt.

"Peter!" Marilyn cried. "Are you hurt?"

"What goes on?" one of the officers asked, collaring two of the surf boys who were trying to slip away.

"They were wrecking Cassandra's house," Marilyn said.

"They grabbed my sister and knocked her down," Peter said, getting shakily to his feet. "They were going to cut off her hair."

"Are you the Buckley kids?" one of the officers asked.

Peter nodded.

"Ward Evans told me you might be down here to lock up." He turned to the surf boys. "Most of the teen-agers we get here are good kids, and the surfers we had last year couldn't have been finer. Then you guys came along. This town's for everybody—not just a few swell-heads who think they can take over. You're going to pack up and get out of town now. C'mon down to the station, you four." And turning to Nico, he said, "If there's any damage in there, ask Mr. Buckley to make a formal complaint and we'll see that these guys pay."

181

As the surfers started up the bank, one of them turned to Nico and muttered, "You stinkin' Greek! You dirty, rotten Greek!"

Peter looked over at Nico. His clothes were covered with sand and mud from the fight.

"You dirty, rotten Greek!" he grinned. And suddenly he and Nico began to laugh until they were both howling.

Marilyn leaned against a rock and looked at her brothers. Even though Peter could not possibly have won a fight with a boy that big, he had leaped right on him to save Marilyn. And Nico had looked mad enough to take on all four boys himself. They really cared about her.

"That was a smart move, Mar," said Peter, still rubbing his neck. "Boy, I'll bet they heard that bell clear down the beach."

"And they couldn't get in to stop her!" said Nico. "I almost laughed except my mouth is full of sand."

"Did they hurt you?" Marilyn asked, worried.

"I am not hurt too much," said Nico. "Are you, Peter?"

"Got a sore shoulder and neck, but I don't think anything's broken," Peter said. "Let's go inside and see what they did."

There wasn't anything that couldn't be cleaned up. Marilyn put the curtains back up and the boys put the pans in the cupboard.

Nico kept chuckling to himself. "You know . . . it

182

really was a funny thing . . . the way they could not get in the house to stop the bell from ringing. They kept running around and around. . . ."

Peter started laughing again too. "I'll bet they were sorry they ever put you in there, Mar," he said.

When all was in order, they checked the screens to make sure they were all locked from the inside, and closed the front door. Father would have to come down and put a new lock on the door before they left.

"Nico," said Marilyn, "I'm sorry about what they called you. . . ."

Nico's eyes sparkled. "Why? It is very funny, really. 'You dirty, rotten Greek,' they say." He looked down at his clothes. "I was clean until I tangle with them. And I am not an apple so it is not possible to be rotten. So I am only Greek, and of that I am glad."

They took off their shoes and waded along the shore, pulling the wagon behind them.

"My head was not quite in place when first I began with those boys," Nico admitted in his strange way of talking. "But . . . I get angry when everyone wants of me all the time . . . when Marilyn says, 'Nico, do this with me,' and Peter says, 'Nico, do that with me.' So one day I see the surf boys riding the waves way down the beach, and I get closer and closer until we are surfing together, you see. They watch me and they say low things I cannot hear, but they do not bother. They watch how I do surfing, and they try to do it same way, and that makes me laugh inside. So whenever I am get tired of only nice

183

things people say to me, I go down to surf with boys and there I must work very hard, for whenever I fall off, the boys laugh loudly. 'Greaseball,' they call me. Do you not understand?"

"I understand," said Marilyn. And she did. At that moment, she felt she understood all the things Cassandra had told her, understood about Ricky, understood about Peter, understood about the ugly old ferris wheel man, understood about love.

15

What the Gulls Were Singing

It was the last day at the beach. The ocean rolled up on the sand, foamy white, leaving frothy bubbles over the castles which were now deserted. The gulls screamed and shrieked and called good-bye.

"I don't wanna go back," Danny said. "Peter and Marilyn and Nico will go to school all day and I won't have anybody—except old Ricky."

"Think what all is going to happen before next summer," said Mother. "There will be Thanksgiving and Christmas, sledding and snowball fights. . . ."

"Have you ever seen snow, Nico?" Marilyn asked.

"A little—in the mountains. But I have never walked in it."

All day long the children carried boxes to the car in the alley. They helped Mrs. Buckley put away sheets and blankets where they would be dry and ready for the opening of Cliff House again next summer.

The guests had all gone now. Many of the other tourist houses were boarded up. The lifeguards were on duty no longer, the teenagers were gone, and the ferris wheel and carousel were covered and locked.

"It looks like a ghost town," said Marilyn, as she and Peter and Nico and Danny took Ricky for a walk in the stroller that afternoon.

They stopped at a window to look at some model boats. Marilyn was barely conscious of two ladies stopping behind her, but their whispers carried to where the children stood.

"That's the baby I told you about, Hattie—the one that's retarded. You can see it in his eyes."

The other lady clicked her tongue. "He belongs to the family that owns Cliff House. What on earth will they do with him?"

Marilyn turned around and faced the women. "Love him," she said quietly, and the ladies stared and moved away.

Supper that evening was on the back porch with everybody sitting on the steps because the chairs had

186

been put away. There were hot dogs and marshmallows and chocolate cookies and pretzels and lemonade.

"Good heavens!" said Mother, looking at the odd assortment of leftovers. "This is a terrible dinner!" But the children loved it.

"Let's all get to bed now," Father said. "We want to get an early start in the morning."

Danny had been promised he could sleep upstairs the last night. When it came time for him to climb in a bed of his own, however, he lost his nerve, and Marilyn let him sleep with her. The Ghost in the Gables must have wanted to make sure he'd be remembered, because he thudded and bumped. Danny pulled his pillow over his head.

"It's only the shutters banging, isn't it, Marilyn?" he whispered.

Marilyn tried to smile in the darkness. "I think the ghost is trying to tell us something," she said. "Hmmmmmm. Clump . . . clumpity . . . clump . . . thump . . . yes, I've got it. He's talking to you, Danny."

Danny scrunched down farther under the covers.

Marilyn put one hand over her mouth to muffle her laughter. "He wants to tell you a secret."

Danny stuck his head out. "What is it?"

"He said to tell you that there is a bottle floating out there on the ocean with our name and address in it. And that if anybody finds it, they will write to us."

"A secret bottle?" asked Danny. "Just like Julius'?"

"Yes, and nobody will know about it except us. Okay?"

187

"Okay," said Danny happily, feeling very big. "Is . . . is the ghost gone now, Marilyn?"

This time Marilyn had to laugh out loud. "Yes, he's gone."

Marilyn didn't know how long she'd been asleep but suddenly someone shook her and she heard her father say, "Quickly! Marilyn! Danny! Get up and come outside. Hurry!"

Marilyn opened one eye. "Is it morning?"

"No. It's midnight. Hurry. Get up."

Father picked up Danny and started downstairs.

"Is the house on fire?" Marilyn asked, tumbling out of bed, and bumping into Nico in the hall.

"No, no. Come out in the yard. I want you to see something."

Marilyn stumbled sleepily out the front door in her robe. Mother reached out for Danny when Father brought him down. "You must see this, Danny! Wake up!" she said. "You will remember it all your life."

The children went curiously out on the porch and down the steps.

"Look!" said Father, pointing to the dark midnight sky.

A streak of yellow light went zooming across the darkness. And then, from a different direction, another.

"What are they, Dad? Rockets?" Peter asked, wide-eyed.

"Shooting stars," said Father. "There are certain

189

times in the year when there are many meteorites in the sky. Tonight was not supposed to be one of them, but you see? There they are." He stopped for a moment and stared silently up at the sky. "Just as there was not supposed to be a hurricane in July, there was one. Just as birds are supposed to sleep at night, can you hear them calling around up there?"

Sometimes meteorites soloed across the sky. Sometimes they seemed to come in pairs. This way and that, little pinpoints of light zipping and zagging. And all the while a gull or two shrieked and called out his sleepy *geeek, geeek* in the dark sky above Cliff House.

It was strange about the gulls. Some of them waddled fat and contented along the boardwalk. Some, like Father, were strictly beachcombers. Some, like Peter and Nico, preferred the water, and spent all their time soaring and diving. And some, like all the Buckley children, would rather be flying around outdoors at night than sleeping like the other birds. But there was a place for each of them at the ocean.

"Do you think they can see the meteorites, too?" Marilyn wondered aloud. "What do you suppose they are singing about?"

This time no one, not even Peter, told her that gulls did not sing. For just as Cassandra could be beautiful, the squawk of the gulls could be a song if someone wanted it to be.

"Perhaps they are scolding us for being out so late," said Mother.

"No," said Father, and he imitated the squeak of the birds. "I think they are saying, 'Now where did I drop that sand crab, Myrtle? I was sure it was right down there.' "

The children laughed.

"Maybe," said Nico, "they sing of the winter to come and the snow that will cover the sand."

They were all wrong, of course, for each gull had a different song. Each belonged to himself and the ocean belonged to all.

The moon was on the water and sand was in the wind. The big black ocean rolled in with a steady *ssslish, ssslish, ssslish.* The sand crabs scurried, the spiders spun, the gulls sang, and the children's hearts beat thud, thud, thud in time with the breakers. Somewhere up in the house, the Ghost in the Gables was clanking out a midnight tattoo. Somewhere, down on the beach, Julius' stump was waiting to be uncovered. Somewhere out on the water, Marilyn's bottle was bobbing up and down, waiting to be found. And somewhere, across the ocean, a girl was waiting to be adopted, and then the Buckleys would be eight. There was so much to come back to next summer.

The night was alive with moving stars and crashing ocean, and Nicolos Panagiotis Buckley and his brothers and sister sat outside in the darkness and listened and looked and wondered.

191